CHURCHYARD ORPHAN

A VICTORIAN CHRISTMAS STORY

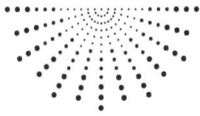

DOLLY PRICE

Publisher's Note: This is a work of fiction. Names, characters, places, and incidents are a product of the author's imagination. Locales and public names are sometimes used for atmospheric purposes. Any resemblance to actual people, living or dead, or to businesses, companies, events, institutions, or locales is completely coincidental.

© 2019 PUREREAD LTD

PUREREAD.COM

CONTENTS

Chapter 1	1
Chapter 2	5
Chapter 3	9
Chapter 4	11
Chapter 5	13
Chapter 6	16
Chapter 7	19
Chapter 8	24
Chapter 9	27
Chapter 10	31
Chapter 11	34
Chapter 12	40
Chapter 13	44
Chapter 14	48
Chapter 15	53
Chapter 16	59
Chapter 17	62
Chapter 18	65
Chapter 19	67
Chapter 20	70
Chapter 21	72
Chapter 22	75
Chapter 23	78
Chapter 24	81
Chapter 25	85
Chapter 26	89
Chapter 27	94
Chapter 28	96
Chapter 29	100
Chapter 30	104
Chapter 31	109

Chapter 32	113
Chapter 33	116
Chapter 34	118
Chapter 35	120
Chapter 36	122
Chapter 37	126
Chapter 38	130
Chapter 39	135
Chapter 40	140
Chapter 41	143
Chapter 42	147
Chapter 43	152
Chapter 44	156
Chapter 45	160
Chapter 46	162
Chapter 47	166
Chapter 48	168
Chapter 49	170
Chapter 50	176
Chapter 51	178
Chapter 52	184
Chapter 53	188
Chapter 54	190
Chapter 55	192
Chapter 56	195
Chapter 57	197
Chapter 58	200
Chapter 59	202
Our Gift To You	209

CHAPTER ONE

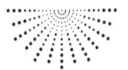

Mrs. Watkins held the wicker basket firmly on her lap as the carriage trundled through the dark streets. A whimper came from within as the wheels went into a rut, and she instinctively steadied it. Her heart beat very fast; she was uneasy about her mission. Peering out the window, she saw a few people, wrapped well against the cold, hurrying from St. Michael's where Midnight Mass was concluding soon; she had not reckoned that anybody would come out before the service ended, but evidently some were in a hurry to get home and enjoy hot mince pies. She wished her husband would hurry the horses and rapped sharply on the roof of the coach as a warning to him.

Now the bells were pealing out Christmas joy to the town. The joy of a newborn Babe, come from

Heaven. She pursed her lips, looking down at the basket. Underneath the loose-fitting lid, a swaddled child lay. An unwelcomed child, only hours old.

The coachman, her husband and conspirator in the business, knew where to stop. She peered out again, holding the basket carefully. She hesitated. Her orders were to leave the basket on the church steps, hide behind a pillar, and make sure somebody saw it and raised the alarm, ensuring the child's safety. But now the crowds were spilling out; she could not leave it unnoticed. Watkins, seeing the problem, urged the horses away a little, toward the churchyard gate a little way down the street. She heard him hop down and he wrenched the door open in haste.

"Mildred," he urged. "It's impossible at the steps. But look – there's a few folks going to the graves. Go and leave it up there."

She got out. She was thankful for a little moonlight, just enough to make out the path between eerie shapes of tall yew trees and rows of headstones.

She walked briskly up the hill feeling hot and panicky in spite of the piercing cold, her husband by her side, carrying a torch which he held low to the ground. They moved between high headstones, furtively, in the general direction of the few lights bobbing in the graveyard as people, having come out from the church, were taking a path to the graves of loved ones.

One light separated from the rest and seemed to be going in a direction which would bring it close to a row of tombstones near an outside wall. Watkins nudged his wife in that direction, and together they turned their steps towards it. Still holding the lamp low, they drew close, until the other lamp came to a standstill. They strained to hear a woman's voice above the bells.

"Are you all right, Mother? You didn't have to come up here with me."

"I'm all right, Jane. Wasn't Johnny a good son-in-law to me? Lay your wreath, we'll say a prayer and go home to our hot cocoa."

The Watkins were only feet away now. Neither of the women had noticed them as their shadowy figures knelt by the graveside. They crossed themselves and began a prayer.

Mr. Watkins signalled to his wife to advance with the basket, in the shelter of the wall, to an overgrown patch of weeds and grasses at the foot of a thick yew. She crept forward, holding the basket carefully. She laid the basket down only ten feet from the women, lifted the lid, and sharply pinched the child's cheek before she scurried off. A wail rose from the basket. Would they hear it, would they, above the bells? She turned her head and saw both women get to their feet in haste.

'A child! Do I hear a child crying? Get the lamp, Jane! Go and see, there by the wall!"

The mission was completed! Mr. Watkins bundled her into the coach and they clattered away as quickly as they could.

CHAPTER TWO

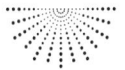

The widow and her mother lost no time in taking the baby home to give her warmth. They laid the basket on the table and as soon as they had lit the lamps and raked up the coals, reopened it.

'EMMA. BORN DECEMBER 24TH *1840'*

"Poor unfortunate mite!" said the older woman, who the townspeople called Grandmother Grey. "Who left 'er there in the cold? Christmas too? She needs heat."

"She's well wrapped up, Mother. See? That's an expensive blanket, I'll say, I haven't had those in the shop this long time. She's no pauper."

Mrs. Grey made herself comfortable by the fireside chair.

"Pick her up and give her to me, Jane. Jane! Support her little head with one hand, and 'er back with the other!"

"Oh Mother, I don't know anything about babies!"

"There, you're all right, but there's no need to hold her out far from yourself like she's a hot saucepan. Be more natural, like. Oh, hold her like you hold that spoiled cat of yours!"

The cat lived in the store room downstairs, and was more of a pet than a working cat.

Jane seemed to understand, and carried the child in a more natural manner. She laid her carefully on her mother's lap, who held her close and rocked her.

Jane looked out the window at the Square, her eyes casting to and fro. "Mother, I saw the lights of a carriage pass the church just as we came out. I wonder if she was brought in that."

"That would fit in with the good blankets about her."

Jane turned again and surveyed the tiny human with anxiety.

"Mother, she needs milk. I don't know the least thing about infants, except that I sell a lot of colic drops!" Jane was now flying about, reaching for a milk-jug and picking up a spoon. "Do I have to warm it?"

"She's not hungry yet. She's very new and won't be hungry for a time. Forget your jug and spoon. That won't do. She needs a wet nurse. The Parish will 'ave to take care of her. She'll 'ave to be reared in the Workhouse."

"Poor little mite. It's Christmas. Mother – I have a mind to keep her, if we could find a mother who would suckle her. Dr. Rogers might know someone, Christmas or no, we'll go to him in the morning."

"Are you sure you want to keep her?" Mrs. Grey's voice was sharp. "Children are a big responsibility. This here is no toy here for you to play with, you know, nor a puppy you might get tired of in January!"

"Phoo, Mother! Don't speak to me as if I'm a child. You know I'll never get married again, at forty, I'm not likely to have a child even if I did. She's a Christmas gift, isn't she? She'll liven up our home, and –" Jane bit her lip, but her mother smiled, guessing her thoughts.

"You won't be alone when I go." said Mrs. Grey. Jane flushed. It had been her very thought. She looked at the head of downy hair and touched it. She'd love this little one as if she was her own.

CHAPTER THREE

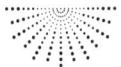

Earlsbury was a growing market town on the London - Oxford road. It boasted a handsome square, several side streets, two churches, an Inn and Stables, tradesmen's shops and a boy's school on the edge of town run by Mr. Groves, who had once been a Latin master in Oxford. Earlsbury was growing and only the year before the railway line had reached it, which boded very well indeed for its future.

Mayfield's Emporium did a brisk trade in all kinds of merchandise. A farmer might get a shovel there, or a young miss a ribbon. A teacher bought his paper, pens and ink; the housekeeper her candles, soaps and scrubbing brushes, the cook her flour and rice. They even had a selection of kid gloves and fur tippets in drawers behind the counter, for some of their clientele were wealthy enough to buy them.

Situated in the main square, the family lived in four rooms above the shop. Up to three years before, Mr. Mayfield, some twenty years his wife's senior, was a fixture behind his counter from early morning until six 'o clock in the evening, until the November day in 1837 when he had dropped dead behind his counter. Since then his widow, aided by her mother who had moved in to help her, had kept the shop open and was doing very well.

Mrs. Mayfield was a clever woman who had a great head for arithmetic, which was why the elderly bachelor shopkeeper had fallen for her. He needed an assistant probably more than he had needed a wife, but Jane relished her role, keeping the books and serving in the shop, while a servant kept the house running upstairs and cooked their meals. The Mayfields had no children, and Jane was too practical to brood over the sorrow. She was not a sentimental person, but even she could not miss the significance of a childless widow finding an abandoned newborn child on Christmas Eve.

Emma was meant to be hers.

CHAPTER FOUR

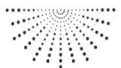

Emma was sent to live with a woman in East Street who had a baby at the breast and plenty of milk. Mrs. Roche brought her daily to the shop to visit and Jane and her mother cooed over her. She was a happy child, and thrived. A year flew by. On Christmas Eve, Jane and her mother went to Midnight Mass. Afterwards, they took the lamp to the graveside of Mrs. Mayfield's late husband. To their surprise, someone had been there before them – and left a parcel wrapped in white paper. Shining the lamp on it, Jane saw 'FOR EMMA' in large letters. She looked about abruptly, vividly recalling the cry from the basket last year, wondering if she was being watched. She took the lamp and shone it about, calling 'Is there anybody there?" above the sound of the Christmas bells. But nobody answered, nor did her lamp reveal anything beyond the walls and the old yews.

The parcel contained a little sprigged muslin dress in white, lined with organdie. Again, Jane noted that the material was not run-of-the-mill.

"Is she gentry, Mother? Maybe a young lady who had her out of wedlock?"

"Oh it doesn't follow that she's gentry." Mrs. Grey frowned. She feared that rearing a child of the gentry would be somehow more challenging. "The mother could be a lady's maid, or works in a draper's shop and gets remnants."

"With a carriage at their disposal, they probably brought her from another town."

Her mother agreed.

CHAPTER FIVE

Emma came to live permanently in the shop the Christmas after she was weaned. Jane employed a nursemaid to look after her while she worked, but as often as not Emma escaped Norah and made her way downstairs, to delight herself in the visual feast that was Aunt Jane's shop. Mrs. Mayfield, though she had given Emma her surname, had decided it was ridiculous to try to pass herself off as her mother, as she had been widowed several years. And when Emma asked questions, she would tell her the truth.

One of her frequent customers was Mrs. Groves, who brought her little boy Andrew, a solemn lad, six years old, with her as she made her purchases. She and Jane were friends of a sort, but Mrs. Groves was the wife of the learned schoolmaster, and thought herself charitable in bestowing her friendship upon a mere shopkeeper's widow. She had a superior way that Jane found irritating.

"Mr. Groves" she said referring to her husband. "could be a Professor today. He could have become a Dean at Oxford, you know. But he preferred to teach younger children, for they are most in need of character formation. He is not ambitious."

"I'm sure he does very well," said Jane, only half-listening.

"Very well! Why of course he does! We are not poor, you know, though our house is small. Now as for Andrew, he will become something. I have great plans for Andrew."

Andrew had picked up a boiled sweet he had found on the floor, and was licking it happily. At that moment, the door from the stairs pushed open and Emma, having once again escaped her captor, toddled in. Seeing another child, she made a beeline for Andrew.

"We must be going." said Mrs. Groves, glancing at Emma.

"But your wax candles –"

"I will send Gracie for them later. Andrew, where did you get that sweet?"

"Off the ground," said her son.

"Drop it at once." said his mother.

Her son looked disappointed, but obeyed. Jane looked annoyed. The front door clanged shut after mother and son. Jane came around the counter and threw away the sweet, resisting Emma's pleas for it. She gathered Emma in her arms and brought her upstairs. She was very irritated at Mrs. Groves and her airs. The way she had looked at Emma! Everybody knew of course that she was a foundling, but that was no reason to be toffee-nosed. Jane wished she could keep Mrs. Groves out of her premises altogether; but Mrs. Groves fancied herself a friend of hers, and she did buy nearly everything for her household there also - Jane was not about to chase away any regular customers.

CHAPTER SIX

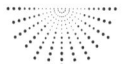

On her fourth Christmas, Emma realised that there was something special about the Season for her, because her birthday was the day before. On Christmas morning, as well as a stocking filled with treats, there was a wrapped gift for her on the living room table. This did not come from Father Christmas, but as Aunt Jane told her that she brought it from Midnight Mass, she asked if it had come from Baby Jesus.

"Of course!" said Mrs. Mayfield, pleased that she did not have to go into the cemetery explanation.

This was the gift that Emma began to look forward to most. Over the next few years, Baby Jesus sent her dolls and sweet little frocks and bows, on what was His Birthday also.

At eight years old, she was old enough to attend Midnight Mass. Before they set out, Mrs. Mayfield told her the truth about her present. Though all presents came from Jesus, she explained, He used other people to deliver them. And this person might leave her present in the churchyard after Mass. Emma, far from being disappointed as she thought she might be, that her gift would not be found in the Crib as she imagined, was very intrigued.

She loved the carols, the church illuminated with candles, and the joyful bells. All enthralled her. "I love Christmas!" she whispered happily to Aunt Jane as they contemplated the peaceful Nativity. "But now can we go to the churchyard to get my present? Please?" She tugged her sleeve.

"Say a prayer first, and we will go." Emma hurried her prayer and gleefully left, holding her aunt's hand tightly. The darkness did not frighten her in the least. They picked their way along the stony path, Aunt shining the lamp until they came to the graveside by the yews and the wall.

"And there's your gift, look!"

Emma exclaimed as she pounced to retrieve the packet wrapped in gold paper.

"And here's where we found you, eight years ago." Aunt Mildred shone her lamp on a thicket of grasses and ferns at the base of the yew tree.

"In the wicker basket?" They still had the lidded basket and the blanket at home.

"In the wicker basket."

"Was I a gift for you and Grandmother Grey, from Baby Jesus?" Emma revelled in the story of how she was found.

"Yes, of course you were." Aunt Jane felt a little glow within her. She'd never regretted keeping Emma. She'd brightened up her life with her smiles and expanded her heart in a way she had not known before. Both she and her mother loved the foundling child.

"Who did Baby Jesus get to give me to you in the basket?"

"I don't know that. You were just there, crying, and we took you home."

"Why was I crying?" Emma seemed sad at this.

"No reason. All babies cry."

CHAPTER SEVEN

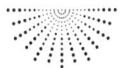

1850

"Father, can we have a Christmas tree? The Williams' have one." Ophelia Groves decided that her father needed prompting. It was after supper and they were all seated by the parlour fire. Her father was cleaning his pipe; her mother was cradling the youngest Groves. Andrew was at the table with the newspaper spread upon it.

"Oh yes, Papa!" Leon, aged four, echoed.

"I do not know about this fad for bringing trees into the house," said their father. "They dry out and I've heard of at least two that have gone on fire, burning the house down."

But his children were united against him.

"Father, the Royal children have a tree at Windsor Castle!" Ophelia cried out.

"They have several, one in each room." Andrew made his contribution.

"Oh, do read it out again!" cried Emilia. Andrew bent to the newspaper and by the light of a wax candle, began to read.

'The Christmas Tree at Windsor Castle.

A Christmas tree is annually prepared, by her Majesty's command, for the royal children. The tree chosen for this season is a young fir, about eight feet high – '

"Tell Papa about the candles and the sweets and the toys on it!" cried Emilia.

"Oh, now I see your object – the tree is to be a receptacle for as many presents as you can possibly fit upon it," said Mr. Groves with amusement. "Mrs. Groves, the avarice of our children at Christmas is a source of constant amazement."

"Oh Mr. Groves, what a thing to say about your own children! If the Royals have a tree, and the Williams, and Miss Shelton is to have a very large one for her nieces and nephews at the Hall, we can have one as well. Everybody has a tree. Would you deny your children one?"

"You misunderstand me, Mrs. Groves. Did I refuse? And I was just joking about avarice, but you fail to see my jests."

Andrew began to read again. *'Fancy cakes, gilt gingerbread, and eggs filled with sweetmeats are suspended by variously coloured ribands...'*

"And an angel at the top!" Emilia interrupted with glee. "Draw it for me, Andrew!" Her brother had a talent for drawing, so a while later he took his paper and pencils and using the newspaper report as a guide, drew the tree at Windsor Castle, making the angel even bigger than he imagined, for the benefit of his little sister and brother who hung on to him at either side, exclaiming and prompting.

The tree arrived the following evening and was decorated over the next few days by the delighted Groves children. Andrew and Ophelia went to Mayfield's shop to buy sweets to wrap up and hang from the tree. They too had caught the fad and a young fir stood in the window, unadorned as yet. The young Groves' described theirs with animation to Emma and Aunt Jane.

"Please show me how to make a decoration!" begged Emma, after he'd told them how they had folded a paper and cut diamond-shapes along the edge, and then shook out the folds.

"Come to our house this evening! We're making twirly ones from silver paper!" cried Ophelia.

"Oh, Aunt Jane, can we go to their house?" asked Emma with eagerness.

"We cannot, my dear. We have too much to do." Mrs. Mayfield knew that Emma would hardly be welcome at the Groves', at least not by Ophelia's mother. "I will show you myself."

In Villiers Street later, Mrs. Groves was annoyed with Ophelia for issuing an invitation to Emma Mayfield.

"She's not our sort, Ophelia. She's a foundling."

"What's a foundling, Mamma?" asked Ophelia, cutting paper for Leon, who was not allowed scissors.

"She was abandoned by her parents as a baby, and the Mayfields found her and took her in."

There followed many curious questions.

"But Mamma, if her mother and father did not want her, should we not show her great kindness?" Ophelia wondered.

"Well of course we should be kind. But we don't want to form a friendship with her. We don't know where she comes from."

"Mamma, does she have any friends at all, then?" Ophelia asked, perplexed.

"Not any respectable ones, I'm sure."

Andrew made no comment, but he felt sorry for Emma. She was a nice little girl and it was a shame that through no fault of her own, she was not allowed to visit them.

CHAPTER EIGHT

By the time she was ten, Emma's questions had become a little deeper. She knew that she did not have a mother or a father, and this fact preoccupied her.

"Why did Jesus tell my mother to give me to you, Aunt?" This was asked with a little resentment.

Aunt Jane understood the natural feeling that prompted the question. Emma had come to feel that she belonged with her mother instead of being given away to a stranger. She took a deep breath.

"Your parents couldn't keep you with them, Emma. Perhaps they were poor, and decided to find another home for you." She clasped her hand tightly as they made their way out of the churchyard, the bells pealing loudly. Emma clutched her gift in her mittened hands. It was the first time the gift had not brought unmitigated excitement.

"So Jesus didn't really send me to you."

"Emma, there are lots of things we don't understand. It's better not to think about them. As for Jesus sending you, every good thing that happens to us happens because of our good God. We won't understand those things until we go to Heaven."

Jane Mayfield had no doubt that a Higher Power existed and ordered the affairs of those who trusted in Him. To her, it was the only way that joys and sorrows made any sense.

"Who are they, Aunt Jane? Who are my mother and father?" There was an intensity in Emma's voice.

"We don't know, Emma."

On Christmas Day Emma was still troubled. Even the present, a fur muff, did not seem to distract her. Grandmother Grey went to an old chest in the corner. There were many items in there that they had no room to display. She unwrapped a large tapestry from its covering of brown paper and brought it to Emma's side.

"Emma, look at it. What's in the picture? Tell me all you see."

"It's a cottage with ivy, and trees on either side, and a garden gate, and rosebushes, and a cat sunning herself on the wall. It's very pretty. But why are you showing me this tapestry?"

Grandmother Grey turned it over.

"Now, what can you see?"

"Nothing much really, only a tangle of coloured threads."

"Yes, only a tangle of threads. Sometimes our lives seem tangled up like that. But God sees the front side. As we will, when we go to be with Him. He'll show us how all our tangles made for a beautiful picture on the right side." She turned it over again.

Emma was silent as she contemplated it.

"Remember that." Grandmother Grey said, putting it away again. "Now, let us sing a few carols; it's Christmas, and we will be joyful today. We have a great deal to be thankful for."

CHAPTER NINE

1852

"You shouldn't eat more sweets than are good for you." Emma teased her customer, as she ladled out a quantity upon the weighing scales.

"I can decide what's good for me." Andy grinned at her.

"You'll rot your teeth and turn your tongue black."

"Who says?"

"The dentist told me. I had to visit him once in Oxford."

"Was it very fearful, the dentist?"

"He took out a tooth, it was so quick it didn't hurt, not at all."

"Really. He took out a tooth! How did he do it?"

"With pliers. One big pull, and it was out!"

"Was there a lot of blood?"

"Oh, yes, lots of it. I was pumping blood all over myself."

Andrew grinned again.

"If you stop selling me sweets, you'll go bankrupt," he said.

"What's bankrupt?"

"You'll get poor. I think I buy enough sweets here to make you rich."

"I am rich already, Master Andrew Groves."

"Are you? Really? How?"

Emma smiled and preened a little. In the last two years, she had often lain awake weaving stories about where she came from. One thing she had decided, her parents were very rich. Last Christmas, she had received several yards of yellow silk – enough for a very pretty summer Sunday dress.

"I don't come from here, you know," she whispered to him over the counter, with a conspiratorial air.

Andrew did not know what to say. He could not repeat what he heard from his mother about Emma Mayfield. Emma was happy and spirited and made him laugh. He liked coming in here, ostensibly to buy liquorice, but really to talk and chat to her. She served a great deal in the shop while her aunt nursed her ailing mother upstairs.

"Where do you come from, then?" he whispered back.

She looked dreamily away, away to a place he did not know. Her violet eyes could be full of thought one minute, then sparkling with fun the next. Now she looked dreamy.

"I was found in the churchyard, in a basket, on Christmas Eve," she said in a great whisper as if ears were everywhere. "My mother was a Princess ballet dancer from Russia. She was dancing in a theatre in London, and was seen by a Lord. He fell instantly in love with her."

Andrew's eyes grew wide.

"After the performance, he went backstage and begged her to marry him. She fell madly in love with him too, and said *Yes*."

Emma paused as a customer came in and asked for an ounce of tobacco. She dealt with him speedily and sent him on his way.

"And then what?"

"She said it would have to be a secret, because he had not asked her father for permission, nor could he ask him, for he was a very old, bad-tempered man."

"Go on," Andrew said, his lips twitching a little.

"So they married in secret. Then, I was born. You see, they could not keep me, because it would be a great scandal, and in the papers, and the Queen would have to be involved, and Tsar Nicholas, and – and diplomats."

"Diplomats. My goodness," Andrew felt like laughing and teasing her about it, but knew he should not. Instead, he felt a great sympathy for this poor girl who did not know where she was from and had dreamed up a romantic story about it.

"I will meet them someday," she said artlessly. "They are still hereabouts, you know."

"Now are you going to give me my liquorice or not?" asked Andrew. He saw Mrs. Mayfield approach; she had heard most of what Emma had said, and was looking at her with some curiousity.

CHAPTER TEN

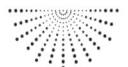

"Emma, I would not think so much if I were you," Aunt Jane challenged Emma after they had closed the shop that evening and were sitting by the fire. Her mother had retired early. "That story I heard you tell Master Andrew – you made it up, and you should not make up stories."

"But how do I know it isn't true, or at least that something like that did not happen?" Emma put down her mending and looked at Mrs. Mayfield. "I know I come from rich people!"

"That might not be so," said her aunt. "Just because they send you a nice gift once a year, doesn't mean they are rich or important or anything. If they were rich, Emma, they would wish you a better life than this one, and provide money for you to be educated, and skilled and accomplished, as young ladies are, so that you could make a good marriage. As it is, Mother has seen to your education as best she could, and I'm teaching you the shop so you will always have a trade if you don't marry."

Emma began to cry.

"But where do they get the money for silk, then?"

"I don't know. Perhaps they save up for it. Emma, don't get your hopes up about your people."

"I don't know where I belong, Aunt Jane," she said in a low tone. "I was thinking – that next Christmas Eve, I could go to the churchyard early and wait – "

"No, I forbid it," Mrs. Mayfield said, sternly.

"You don't know how hard it is not to be able to call somebody *'Mamma'*." Emma lamented.

Mrs. Mayfield wanted to get up from her chair and embrace her, but displays of affection were not her way. So she leaned forward and said to her with earnestness: "Emma dear, you would be disappointed. If they did not wish to keep you, or could not keep you, twelve years ago, it may be the same way now. They know where you are, or how to find you, and yet they do not attempt it."

"I am so unhappy!" cried Emma, getting up from her chair and rushing to her room. She flung herself on her bed and cried bitterly.

Mrs. Mayfield came and stood at the door.

"I wish I could have been your mother, Emma, if that's any comfort. But look at me – I can't even embrace you as a mother should!" Tears stood in her eyes.

Emma sprang from her bed and threw her arms about Mrs. Mayfield, startling her.

"It doesn't matter," she said. "You have been my mother. What would have happened to me, if you hadn't found me? I might have starved or been eaten by wolves!"

The older woman's arms found their way around her foster child at last in an affectionate clasp.

"What an imagination, child! There are no wolves left in England these four hundred years! Go on to bed, and I will bring you some warm milk."

CHAPTER ELEVEN

1854

Mrs. Grey died in early January. Emma grieved for the old lady who had taken her to her heart. She wondered if she had any grandmother living and if so, what she was like.

Mrs. Mayfield and Emma kept the house and shop going between them. The large account books in the back befuddled Emma, but she excelled at selling. She had a bright and engaging personality and customers took to her. Andrew, a day pupil at his father's school, often sauntered in to buy the liquorice he was fond of, and while he was there offered help in lifting and carrying items that were heavy and bulky, which both Mrs. Mayfield and Emma were often glad to accept.

"He has a good, kind nature," Mrs. Mayfield said. "He didn't get it from his mother."

One day he had with him his paper and pencils, and mentioned that he was learning portraiture. Emma asked him to sketch Bunty, the cat. Bunty objected to being stared at, and got up and stalked away, but not before Andrew had managed to get a good likeness of him. Emma chuckled at the portrait. Andrew had perfectly captured Bunty's hostile manner.

Business was brisk on Market Day in late September. The shop was busy from early morning. Usually, Mrs. Groves did not venture out of her home in Villiers Street on Market Day, disliking the bustle and the smells of the animals, the soiled streets and what she called *'the rough element'* that frequented town on these days. Mrs. Mayfield was therefore surprised to see her come into the shop and patiently wait her turn behind two chattering farmers' daughters who had a great deal of trouble making up their minds about ribbons. Emma took over serving them, briskly told each what suited her, and they left a few minutes later, with much chatter about the possibility of encountering some young men known to them if they took one street rather than another.

Mrs. Groves looked after them.

"Common girls! I would not like my girls to behave so in public."

"How may I serve you today?" Mrs. Mayfield asked. She was impatient. She and Emma would have to haul some flour bags from the store at the back while there was a lull. Emma was arranging the ribbons back in the drawer in some sort of order.

"Did you get any of Browne's Almond soap that I like?"

"No, but I have the Pears Transparent." Jane replied. Had Mrs. Groves braved the vulgar masses for a bar of toilet soap instead of sending her servant? But no. The schoolmaster's wife had a gleam in her eye, and Mrs. Mayfield knew that she wished to impart some intelligence.

"Oh dear, it does not suit my skin as much. It's cheaper of course. But I will take a half pound."

"Very well. That's sevenpence please."

"I suppose you have heard the news, Jane." she said casually, as Mrs. Mayfield wrapped her soap in a piece of paper.

"About the cholera in London? Is it not dreadful? Ten thousand dead! It's the pump water that's dirty; Mr. Roche told me."

"Oh that is dreadful, but no, some news that is closer to us here in Earlsbury."

"I haven't heard anything." Mrs. Mayfield tried to keep the impatience from her voice. Yet, she was very curious.

"You know that Hatters Building has been sold."

This building was located across the square, and had been a warehouse. It had lain empty for some time.

"I heard that, but as to whom, I haven't heard."

"Mr. Groves has been told by Mr. Williams that it has been sold to Baggotts of Birmingham." Mrs. Groves said with some triumph.

"Baggotts of Birmingham." Mrs. Mayfield took in this information, but said nothing at first. Baggotts were very successful merchants. Their shop in Birmingham was vast, three houses in one and three floors in each house – the family lived in a mansion outside town. Baggotts had a reputation for undercutting smaller competitors, putting them out of business. Emma, her fingers folding a length of purple ribbon, looked anxiously at her aunt.

"Well, you do know that the old Mr. Baggott, who began it all, has three sons. The eldest is being sent here to open a branch." Mrs. Groves went on.

"I daresay we will bear the addition," Mrs. Mayfair said bravely. "Earlsbury is growing apace. I am not afraid of a little competition. These big shops can be bewildering to customers, and many prefer the personal service offered in smaller establishments, so I'm sure it will make little difference to us."

"That is good, then." Mrs. Groves made for the door, forgetting her purchase.

"Oh, Mrs. Groves – your soap." Emma called after her. "And – Master Andrew left his pencil here yesterday, it's a good one, I think he would miss it. We have kept it for him."

"Andrew? Was he here?" Mrs. Groves looked displeased.

"Well, yes." said Emma lamely. Mrs. Groves, she knew, did not like her, she treated her differently because she was a foundling. She blushed and looked down. Mrs. Groves looked at her for a long moment, and with a swish of her skirts made for the door and left, banging the door after her.

Mrs. Mayfield was very quiet, staring into space.

"Will Baggotts of Birmingham affect us, Aunt?" asked Emma, turning her thoughts to the news that Mrs. Groves had delivered.

Mrs. Mayfield nodded dumbly. She seemed to be in a trance for the rest of the day. Emma dealt with the customers with efficiency and cheer, trying not to be fearful of what was to come.

CHAPTER TWELVE

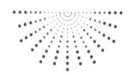

"Andrew, I must speak with you. Emilia, go and find something to do elsewhere." Mrs. Groves appeared in the parlour, shooing her younger daughter who was sitting with her embroidery. She sat down opposite him.

"What is it, Mother?" He put down the paper.

"Do you frequent Mayfield's very often?"

The direct nature of the question made him uneasy. His mother seemed to be accusing him of something.

"Frequent? Whenever I need something, Mother."

"I really would prefer if you stayed away from that place. That girl Emma has her eye upon you. She spoke of you in such a familiar, intimate way, that it was obvious she thinks she has your affections."

"Mother, please do not say that." Andrew coloured a little, making his mother examine his countenance deeply.

"Yes, she spoke of you in a very common way too. You left a pencil after you yesterday. Why would you use your pencil in the shop, unless you were sketching to pass the time there? What, or who, were you drawing?"

Andrew said nothing, only got up and looked out the window.

"Mother, I'm not a child anymore. There is no need to speak to me as you do. I am master of my own affairs, and of where I wish to spend my money. I go there sometimes to buy this or that, and I occasionally make a little sketch there of some object of curiousity. Yesterday, it was the cross old cat Bunty. And I sometimes assist Mrs. Mayfield and Emma if they need help with heavy lifting." He said this because he knew it would get to his mother's ears anyway.

"Andrew! You lift and carry, like a common apprentice?"

"It's Christian charity, Mother."

"They are using you! What if anybody saw you? You and all of us will be a laughing-stock! I must speak to you frankly, Andrew. Your father and I have a future planned for you. You are to become somebody, and some harlot's daughter is not going to ensnare you into marriage and hold you back."

"Mother!" he wheeled around, horrified. "Emma Mayfield is a sweet, innocent girl. She has nothing like that upon her mind. She's not even fifteen, as far as I know. And surely you don't suspect me of some kind of lechery! Your words seem to imply that!"

"Forgive me, Andrew. But even girls of fifteen have been known to fall with child, and ruin the lives of young men like you. Thankfully you are to go up to Oxford soon, there you will meet a very different set of people than you are used to here. Your father had no ambition, so all my hope rests in you to raise us in society, so that your sisters can make advantageous marriages, and we can move from this little house so irritating to me. Is that understood?"

He made no reply, only bit his lip, silently fuming. The he turned and walked from the room, angrily.

'It will be all moot, in any case' Mrs. Groves said to herself. *'When Baggotts of Birmingham opens up,*

Mayfield Emporium will be finished in Earlsbury, and they will have to remove themselves elsewhere.'

Andrew left the house. His mother's mind was a nest of wicked suspicion. He went to an alehouse and drank with a few farm labourers who with their easy banter made him forget his mother and her hollow ambitions.

CHAPTER THIRTEEN

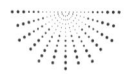

C hristmas approached. Emma loved decorating the window beforehand, with sparkly baubles and paper decorations and red-berried holly twined around the toys and gifts on display. On this Monday morning, however, as she worked, she could not but see the procession of carts that came from the Railway and stopped outside what had been Hatter's Building. A crowd gathered to watch the teams of men as they shouldered carpets and furniture inside, and a ripple of awe went through the spectators as a piano was hoisted to the windows on the upper floors.

"They'll sell everything from a needle to an anchor," enthused Miss Shelton, who was one of their regulars and being served at the counter at that very moment. "But I won't darken their doorstep," she added quickly. "My family has always done business at Mayfields."

"Rest assured, Mrs. Mayfield," said old Mr. Hawkins a little bit later who as landlord of the Earlsbury Inn was one of their best customers, "that I will continue my patronage here. The association between our families goes back several generations. You will receive our monthly orders for supplies as usual, Mrs. Mayfield." But Emma frowned. She noticed his son was across the road, talking with animation with a gentleman who was there every day, overseeing the move. She had been told that it was young Mr. Baggott.

Baggotts of Birmingham opened two weeks later. An ostentatious Christmas Display in their window ensured that shoppers dawdled there. The Mayfields watched in dismay as their customers, even Miss Shelton who had declared that she'd never darken their doorstep, entered the larger Emporium. Miss Shelton emerged with several dozen packages carried by assistants to her waiting carriage. The monthly order arrived from Earlsbury Inn, but they required no candles or lamp oil.

"What will we do, Aunt?" asked Emma on Christmas Eve when they shut the shop and went upstairs to a supper prepared by their maid Sarah. Much of their

Christmas merchandise had been left unsold, and the strains of merry carol singers only seemed hollow to Emma. It was her birthday, but she did not feel very happy, and she knew Aunt Jane was putting on a cheerful front.

"We will not think about that until after Christmas," she said firmly. "We celebrate your Birthday and that of Our Lord. Are you going to wear your new hat to Midnight Mass?"

Aunt Jane's birthday gift was a cheery scarlet bonnet trimmed with black bows and ribbons. But Jane knew that Emma's mind was upon her *other* birthday gift. It preoccupied her every year.

After Mass, they went to the grave as usual, and a small package awaited Emma there. At home, she unwrapped it, to find a little box with a gold locket on a chain within. Her eyes leaped with excitement. She took it out with feverish hope and prised the sides apart with eagerness, expecting to see a miniature of her mother or her father, but it was empty.

"I will put your miniature in there, Aunt." she said with stoicism, but bitterly disappointed.

"That would be very nice, Emma. But I never had my likeness taken." Silently, Mrs. Mayfield was angry with Emma's relatives. Who would have been so carelessly inconsiderate? Did they not know how the child longed to know who she was, how her little fingers would have opened the locket with hope?

"I don't know whether Christmas is a happy time for me," Emma mused, putting the locket away in its green velvet box. "It makes me feel that out in the world, there are people thinking of me, but I must not think of them! Aunt, I like your gift much better than this. And you love me more than they do."

"You were my Christmas blessing, and still are," her aunt said warmly, and with a little discomfort, as she rarely said anything affectionate. Her love for Emma was expressed in making her comfortable and happy and trying to keep her feet on the ground when she went into flights of fancy about her relations. She was growing into a beautiful girl, with wide violet eyes and dark hair in ringlets about her heart-shaped face. Mrs. Mayfield felt that she would always need a practical person to take care of her.

But what of the shop? What would happen to them now?

CHAPTER FOURTEEN

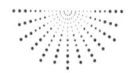

The year was difficult, but they kept going. Even Emma longed to see the inside of Baggotts, but she would not go over there for fear of hurting her Aunt. She'd heard that there were pulleys conveying money to the offices above, and that change and a receipt was put in there and sent back to the cashier and customer.

She was worried about Aunt Jane. She suffered from headaches and her sight was becoming bad, and she could not see the figures in her books. Spectacles did not help, and the doctor told her she might need an operation, which frightened her very much.

"Emma is a bright girl," Mrs. Mayfield confided one day to Andrew, who was now a firm friend of the establishment, his mother's opposition only fuelling his determination to be of use to them. "But she has no head at all for figures! Though she is not unintelligent; ask her to repeat anything she has read, and she can relate it to you with hardly an error! And the stories she makes up for the children when they come in, about the merchandise coming to life at night and dancing at a Ball."

Andrew thought this was marvellous.

He offered to help with the account-keeping, so one evening they brought the ledgers upstairs to give Emma a lesson in arithmetic. He groaned when he opened the ledger.

"What's the matter?" asked Emma, her elbows on the table, her curls falling over her face.

"It's –em - rather a mess, that's what. You have crossed out this, and wrote over it – and what's that ink-blob?"

"My first total was wrong, so I crossed it out and wrote the correct figure over it, and then I was thinking, and the ink dropped from my pen. I blotted it with paper, but it ended up looking like a butterfly."

"Thinking? Dreaming, more like." smiled Mrs. Mayfield, folding clothes. She could see enough to do many tasks that did not need her to read.

"Don't you think it looks like a butterfly?" Emma asked Andrew.

"Yes, it is a butterfly, but that's not going to help you with your arithmetic."

"Oh, no – of course not." Emma frowned, pursed her lips in concentration, and bent her head to the book.

"When you have twenty figures to add, do them first on a separate sheet of paper. That way, you will not have crossings out and errors in your book, and big blobs of ink, as you have. "The easiest way to do that is, add the first two figures, then add the third to the total of the first two, and so on…"

Emma began to learn from him, and Andrew checked the books often. He was very pleased with her progress, for she was really trying, and when she put her mind to something, she could do it well enough.

"No more butterflies, I see," he said, smiling as he closed the ledger the following month.

"I thought my Incoming Total for the month was wrong, though." Emma said. "Would you mind checking it? It couldn't be as low as that, even if Mr. Hawkins from the Inn doesn't trade with us at all now. He is completely gone over to Baggotts."

Andrew was silent as he added the figures.

"It's correct, in fact." he said. Emma turned her violet eyes on him.

"But we've lost a great deal of money, if that's the case," she said, troubled. "Aunt Jane says we'll have to borrow money to keep going."

"Would you come to the Bank with me, Andrew?" Aunt Jane asked quietly. "I would appreciate your assistance. What a Cross not to be able to read! What shall we do when you are gone to Oxford? When are you going?"

"In under six weeks."

"What are you going to do there?" Emma asked.

"Mostly Classical Literature. Drawing too, I hope."

"You mean books? Like Shakespeare? We read a volume of Shakespeare last year, did we not, Aunt? I thought it funny! He called somebody *a Banbury cheese*!"

They all laughed. Andrew, who had not before now thought of Emma as anything other than a child, saw that she was growing up into a lovely young woman. Tonight her hair was up, showing her heart-shaped face to advantage. When she smiled, she showed dimples. Her figure was neat and womanly. But he must not begin to think about Emma Mayfield. He was going to Oxford, where he would be expected to make the acquaintance of rich young men who would introduce him to their sisters. He would miss the Mayfields though. There was a contentment to be found with them that he did not have at home. His parents quarrelled all the time, his mother constantly complaining that his father had no ambition; his father arguing that she did nothing except nag him. He was caught in the middle, and he looked forward to leaving home.

CHAPTER FIFTEEN

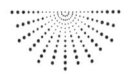

Business on the second Christmas since Baggotts had opened was worse than the first. This time their window display was a revolving tree, showing twinkling gas-lights and shiny objects. Toys were strewn on the floor in all their glory for children to long for – dolls, tops, hula hoops, rocking horses, shuttlecocks, soldiers.

As Christmas Eve approached, Emma was preoccupied by her usual thoughts. Where did she come from? Who had left her in the churchyard? She burned to go there.

Mrs. Mayfield was feeling unwell with a cold, so she went to bed early and would not go out that evening. Emma's heart leaped as she saw her chance. When she was sure saw that her aunt was comfortably asleep, she sat at the table and wrote a note. She hesitated over it, crumpled the first one, and wrote another.

Dear Mother, I assume it is you I must thank for your gifts. Why do you not make yourself known to me? Your loving daughter, Emma.

She wrapped herself in her cloak, and taking her muff, she set out for the cemetery about ten o'clock. She hoped she would be in time. Only the street lights lit her way as she slipped in the gate and made her way up to Mr. Mayfield's grave, past the yews and the headstones, some awkwardly crooked among the straight. She was not late, for there was nothing there yet. She placed the envelope where her gift was always set down, and then moved away a little, sitting on a low wall surrounding another plot, shielded from view.

It was cold! She felt her feet become numb. She got up to move a little, but dropped down suddenly as the lights and sounds of a carriage bobbed along the quiet street. It was not slowing – yes – it was! It was going past the gate – no – it was halting! She heard the gate's long squeak as it opened. Her heart began to thump in her chest. Her face became cold, her hands inside her muff trembled as her ear caught the rhythm of footsteps crunching on the path. Closer,

closer. Louder, louder. She hardly dared to breathe! A light bobbed, carried low. A figure in a top hat and greatcoat came out of the darkness. A man! Not her mother, then! Her father, maybe? Please let him be her father! She watched him pass the spot where she had hidden herself. He carried something.

Emma saw him bend and take up the envelope, then look around. Her heart was bursting with longing. She could bear it no longer! She sprang to her feet.

"Who's there?" said the man, wheeling around.

"It's Emma Mayfield."

"You shouldn't 'ave come, Miss."

"Why not? The packet you're holding in your hand is for me, isn't it? There has been one for me every year for the last fifteen years!"

"You shouldn't 'ave come, Miss."

"Why not? Who are you?"

"I can't tell you, Miss."

"You must tell me! Please! You don't know how I've lain awake nights wondering who I am! It's breaking my heart! Are you my father?"

"No, I am not, Miss. Here, take this box, with the compliments of your benefactor."

"Benefactor! I don't want a benefactor! I want my family! Parents!"

He set the gift upon the grave, as he had done for many years.

She rushed to retrieve it, and shoved it back into his gloved hands.

"Take it. I don't want it. I never want to hear from them again. Tell them that!"

She burst into sobs and ran away, down the path, hardly caring if she tripped and hurt herself. Out the gate she went, and glanced at the carriage in the light of the street lamp. There was no insignia, nothing to indicate who it belonged to. The messenger was also the coachman, for there was nobody else about. Unless there was someone in the carriage! She wrenched open the door.

There was nobody inside. She ran away. At the end of the street, she bumped into somebody on the corner. She felt herself held by strong hands.

"What the – it's Emma! Emma! What can be the matter?" Andrew was holding her, and she was sobbing freely.

"Come on, I'll walk you home. You can tell me about it on the way."

But Emma would not speak. She'd stopped crying, but every few moments a choking sob burst from her, making him very concerned. He asked her if she had been attacked, or if a man had taken some liberty, or if she had lost something important, and to all of these she shook her head. He saw her into the shop and up the stairs, where she lit a candle with shaking hands. She seemed to be in another world.

"I will leave you if you wish," he offered.

"Please do."

"If there's anything I can do –"

"There is nothing, nothing anybody can do!"

The door opened, and Aunt Jane stood here, a shawl wrapped tightly about her.

"Emma," she said in a disappointed tone. "Please tell me you didn't go to the churchyard to try to meet -."

"I did. And a man came. I thought it might be my father but he said he wasn't. He scolded me for being there, trying to find out – who I was – and he put the gift into my hands, and I gave it back to him, and

I told him I never wanted to hear from – those people – again!" She burst into fresh tears.

"The churchyard?" Something stirred in Andrew's memory, something he had not thought about for quite some time. Emma had been found in a graveyard. He looked quizzically at Mrs. Mayfield.

"Someone leaves a birthday gift there for her every year," she explained. "I told her not to try to find out who it was. I was so afraid this would happen." She stood and looked at the sobbing girl with concern, and Andrew realised that she was not about to embrace her. He turned and took Emma in his arms. It was a liberty, but he strongly felt that she needed someone to hold her.

"There, there." he said. "Weep as much as you like, you have reason enough. But I don't like to see Emma miserable. I came home from Oxford to see you."

He had not meant to say that, but there it was. Mrs. Mayfield smiled to herself.

"I'm going back to bed." she said. "Don't keep her up too long, Andrew. We are going to Church early tomorrow."

CHAPTER SIXTEEN

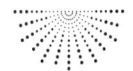

A few days later, Andrew paid a social call to the apartments. Aunt Jane had gone to take mince pies to a poor old lady she knew, so Emma was alone.

"I see you brought your sketch book," she said. "Bunty is asleep, and doesn't look very interesting." She shyly met his eye, the remembrance of his embrace in her distress was a sweetness to her, more than she wanted him to know.

"I wonder, if you - would – would sit for me?" he asked Emma, a little embarrassed. To his relief she immediately accepted.

"All right! Where?"

"Just sit over by the window, where the light is falling on you. Turn a little to the left. Perfect."

He worked for about a half an hour, she gazed at the wallpaper with admirable patience, then he showed it to her.

"My eyes are not that wide." she said.

"They are, and beautiful too."

"My mouth is bigger than you have made it."

"No, your mouth is just like a rosebud; I was thinking of a rosebud." Andrew blushed furiously, but grinned happily.

"Do you like the expression in your countenance?" he had asked her then.

"Yes, I suppose I do."

"I was trying to capture innocence, and something of the longing that I know to be in your heart. I hope you don't mind."

"No, not at all." Emma examined it with more interest. Andrew knew, and accepted, the grief in her heart. It touched her.

"Perhaps, in ten years, you will allow me to do another, and you will have an expression of great contentment."

"I hope so! In ten years, maybe I will have found out something about myself."

'And in ten years', Andrew said to himself, *'Maybe we will be married.'*

CHAPTER SEVENTEEN

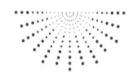

It was February. Aunt Jane's cold had lingered, and before long had turned into a chest inflammation, and she was ill much of the time. Emma ran the shop. She'd enlisted a neighbour, Mickey, to help her with the heavy work. He was a good lad.

One morning, Mrs. Groves opened the door of the Mayfield Emporium. She had only that day found out from Ophelia that Andrew had visited the Mayfields more than once at Christmas, and she was very angry. For the first time since Baggotts of Birmingham had opened in Earlsbury, she entered the Mayfield premises. She hardly noticed the reduced merchandise, the emptied shelves, and its general air of collapse. All she saw was the girl behind the counter, the girl from the very dregs of society to whom she had come to issue a severe warning.

"Good morning, Mrs. Groves." Emma said, feeling a familiar discomfort in her presence.

"Do not *'good morning'* me, Emma. I have something to say to you and you had better listen. It's about my son. Stay away from him. If you have any regard for him, you will not ever see him again. You are not of his rank, and must drag him down. I am sorry to put it like that but it is better to be blunt about such matters as this. And besides, he does not think as much of *you* as you might think. My boy is uncommonly intelligent and gentlemanly, and in his college in Oxford are peers – the sons of great men in the City - who have taken a liking to him, and he has more invitations to their country estates than he can ever fulfil. There is one peer – he has already visited him, and has met his sister – but I need say no more, except for this - in his last letter to me, my son indicated that he has formed an attachment and expects to become engaged soon. If he has led you to believe that he feels something for you, I would advise you to ignore it, for it will all end in great disappointment for you. Have I made myself clear?"

Emma was rooted to the spot. She was robbed of speech. As Mrs. Groves had made her oration, her mind had been filled with so many emotions that she could hardly take in what she was hearing. Andrew had implied – but never said - that he loved her. The day of the portrait had had a great feeling about it; he had embraced her again, and kissed her before he left, and her heart had done several little leaps. He had departed as if reluctant to leave, clasping her hand as if he could not bear to let it go.

And she missed him.

Then Andrew had gone back to Oxford, and forgotten her. And now, Andrew was going to marry this other girl, way above her!

She nodded, without words. Mrs. Groves left the shop.

Mickey came out from the back.

"That ould wagon!" he said. "I heard it all. I hope you didn't believe a word she said! She was tryin' to put you off, that's what! And she didn't buy as much as a matchstick!"

But Emma thought that if Andrew did not come back to Earlsbury for his Easter holidays, then what his mother said must be true.

CHAPTER EIGHTEEN

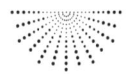

Easter came, bringing sunshine and glorious spring flowers to Earlsbury, but no Andrew. It must be true, then. Emma felt dejected, but perhaps it was for the best. There was another young man, George Phillips, who was paying her attention. George was a coachmaker's apprentice and had a jolly way about him, constantly joking and bantering. But even George's mother did not like her, she felt.

The improved weather did not return Aunt Jane to health. The doctor visited frequently and prescribed a myriad of tonics and treatments for her chest. She was too stoic to lay upstairs, so as often as not she was in the shop with Emma. But when she was forced to lie in bed, Aunt Jane's thoughts were of Emma's future. At sixteen, she was old enough to form an attachment, and though it would be full young to marry, having a man by her side would afford her protection and security in a world that in many ways had been cruel to her. But it would, of course, have to be a good, kind man who loved her deeply. She had thought Andrew Groves would be the man, but as had happened many a young man before him, his head had evidently been turned by seeing a more genteel world. She did not like young Phillips as much, but there were other fish in the sea.

She hoped she would live long enough to see Emma settled, and she had an idea about how to turn the business around too. They would go into Drapery and Haberdashery, and stock the finest linens, laces and sewing supplies for miles around. They would become exclusive. Her debts were immense, but she would turn it around with hard work and prudence. As soon as she felt better, she would begin.

CHAPTER NINETEEN

Dear Mother and Father, as you've indicated I am not to return home for Easter, I have elected to accept an invitation to Lord Edison's home in Norfolk. I have never seen that part of the country, so it should be interesting. I hope you are all well. I hope you will not stop me from coming home in summer, indeed – you must not. Give my love to all, your son Andrew.

"What is this, Amelia?" Mr. Groves was very annoyed. "Why are you keeping him away?"

"It's Emma Mayfield, isn't it?" said Ophelia. "He likes her, and she likes him, and it cannot be!"

"Surely that's not sufficient excuse to stop him from coming home to the bosom of his family for the greatest Christian Feast of the year!"

"You will see the wisdom of what I'm doing in a very short time, Charles. What is so wrong with wanting your eldest son to marry well? He can just as easily fall in love with the daughter of a Lord or a Lady, as with a Miss Emma Mayfield who is the daughter of nobody. Admit it, husband, you would not wish the connection, would you?"

"No," he admitted after a pause. "I would not."

"I knew you would see sense," declared his lady. "Now who are the Edisons? How annoying he tells us nothing of them! Philly, go and fetch me the Peerage."

Ophelia went to the bookcase and took down the large volume.

"He will hardly go to Norfolk for the summer, since he has been asked for Easter – but we must keep him away from here – so I think it would be a very great opportunity for him, were he to go abroad in the summer holidays. Just think, Switzerland!"

"Oh, Mother! Why do we not all go? Father! We are not so poor as to be unable to take a holiday, are we?" Ophelia jumped up, followed by her sister Emilia.

"Why that is the best idea we have had for a very long time!" said Mrs. Groves, rapidly turning the pages of the Peerage.

"But we cannot afford it."

"Borrow, dear. What are banks for? We need not take an expensive house, and can cook for ourselves, so that will be a saving."

"I have never seen the Alps!" mused Mr. Groves. "I think we might, after all! What an experience it would be! The Lakes are said to be magnificent!"

"That settles it then!" cried his wife. She heaved a great sigh of relief. She was sure that by year's end, the Mayfields would have left Earlsbury, for everybody knew that their business was doing very badly indeed.

CHAPTER TWENTY

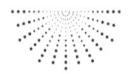

Mrs. Groves was gratified to see Emma Maybury one evening in the company of a young man. Everything was going her way, after all! But just in case, she needed to pay another visit to Mayfield Emporium. Her summer plans were to be bragged about everywhere.

Mrs. Mayfield was behind the counter this time with Mickey assisting her.

"We are off to Switzerland for the summer," she said. "We have decided to take a chalet by Lake Geneva. It will be a perfect opportunity for the girls to learn German, and Andrew of course will accompany us."

"That will be an opportunity indeed," said Mrs. Mayfield. She was feeling tired and unwell, but kept her best side out.

"I saw Emma with a young man the other evening," said Mrs. Groves, rather slyly. "I am glad for her. A coachman would be a good catch for her."

"I'm sure Emma does not set out to catch anybody at all, Mrs. Groves." the reply was icy.

"All the same, Jane, you must worry about her. She has no background, so if I were you, I would encourage this attachment. It would not be every young man who would accept a girl such as Emma. You know well of what it is I speak."

Mrs. Mayfield felt a rising anger.

"Emma is my responsibility," she snapped. "Do I tell you how to raise your children?"

"Indeed, no, and I would take great offense if you did."

"Then you will kindly keep your opinions about Emma to yourself. Now, do you want to buy something, or did you just come in to inform me of your plans for the chalet by Lake Geneva?"

"Some people are too mean-spirited to hear the good fortune of others." Mrs. Groves stalked away.

CHAPTER TWENTY-ONE

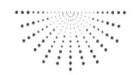

Emma was very disappointed to hear that Andrew would not be in Earlsbury for the summer, and recognising her own feelings for him, ended her courtship with Mr. Phillips, for whom she cared little after the first few weeks. He did not seem to mind the parting, and had a Miss Smith on his arm the following week.

She was becoming worried about Aunt Jane, whose cough was ongoing. But Mrs. Mayfield assured her that her illness was just temporary, and that sufficient rest and nourishment would restore her to health. And during the summer, the cough disappeared completely.

"There, Emma. I told you it would leave me. Now, we are to make plans, and I will need your help. We will turn this business around, you'll see."

But her vision was deteriorating. Aunt Jane was still very frightened of an operation to remove the cataracts and put it off.

"I will have it done in the New Year," she pledged Emma.

But it was not to be. One morning in November, Emma woke up to Sarah's screaming. She jumped out of bed and ran to her Aunt's room. Sarah, bringing Mrs. Mayfield her morning cup of tea, had found her dead upon the pillow.

Emma threw herself upon the lifeless form, sobbing, entreating her to wake up, not to leave her, yet knowing that it would not be. The doctor came and declared that she had had a heart attack.

"The coughing weakened her heart," he said. "I am sorry, Miss Emma. But she did not suffer, and you can take comfort in that."

Emma stroked the still, white forehead of the woman who had been a mother to her, talking to her, her heart filled with abject grief. Over the next days, many of the townspeople came to pay their respects, but she was very frightened of what would happen next, and longed to see Andrew Groves among the sea of visitors. But he did not come.

CHAPTER TWENTY-TWO

"You do understand, Miss, that though Mrs. Mayfield left you all in her will, that there is a great debt attached, and that it would be in your interest to allow Baggotts of Birmingham to absorb Mayfield Emporium and the debts with it. That will relieve you of any risk of having to give yourself up to the mercy of your creditors, who could go to court and get an order against you."

"I understand," Emma said, thoroughly frightened at his words. She felt very strange sitting in this office that smelled of leather and old books, with the bald man opposite telling her that she was bankrupt. She remembered where she had first heard the word, from Andrew, and how they had laughed over it.

Where was Andrew? What his mother had said must be true, for he had not been in contact with her since Aunt Jane had died. It did not occur to Emma that Mrs. Groves had been very careful to keep that knowledge from him.

"I'm not at all sure that you do," Mr. Williams said. "Baggotts of Birmingham have made you an offer for the ailing business, will repay the Bank, and you are left with nothing, but it is better than having to go to Debtor's prison."

"Debtor's Prison!" Emma was shocked into understanding. She nodded her head. It was galling to have to give the Emporium to those who had ruined her and Aunt Jane, but there was no other choice.

"They will give you one week to gather your personal effects and leave the premises. There will be Evaluators and Inspectors around to look at the merchandise, furniture etcetera, and remove it."

"I have nowhere to go," Emma said, helplessly. He looked at her keenly.

"You might, Miss Mayfield, consider seeking a position at Baggotts of Birmingham. They employ a few females in their Ladies Department, and provide accommodation."

"Work for them when they ruined my beloved aunt? Oh no, Mr. Williams. I could not ever work for them."

"Then I am sure you have friends who will shelter you, Miss Mayfield." Emma was silent. She had never had friends from merchant families, for her low beginnings ensured that mothers kept their daughters away from her. She had friends among the servants of the town, but none of them would be able to take her in. No, there was nobody to whom she could turn. She thought briefly of Ophelia Groves, who had always been friendly to her. They were back two months from their summer holidays, but apart from seeing her at her aunt's funeral, she had not had any opportunity to talk to her. Besides, Ophelia perhaps thought of her now as her mother did – an inferior creature.

Mr. Williams did not want to be concerned any more with Miss Mayfield's welfare. Baggotts had made him a generous offer to sway all in their favour. So he produced the forms she was to sign, and calling his clerk to witness, he placed them before her one by one. Emma signed them all.

CHAPTER TWENTY-THREE

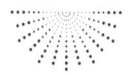

Two days later, agents from Baggotts of Birmingham's came through the shop, the storeroom and the apartment upstairs like an army of busy ants. Emma watched the invaders with alarm. They took no notice of her except to demand keys to the bureau and to be led to where the ledgers were kept. One of them took them all away, staggering under their weight as he carried them out the door.

"Miss Emma, Mickey and I need our wages, go get all the money from the till afore they take that too!" Sarah hissed in her ear and practically pushed her downstairs. She emptied the till, paid Sarah and Mickey, and counted what was left over – six shillings and eightpence-halfpenny. She remembered a small collection of sovereigns and guineas that her aunt kept in a jug on her bedchamber mantel. She took it away. That was what she had to live on! And she had reason to be very grateful to Sarah, for a man opened the till and slammed it shut again when he found nothing there, casting her an accusing glance. She quickly realised that she had to get everything she owned into hiding, for there were carts drawing up outside the door and furniture was being carried out, where would they stop? She got a box and stuffed her clothes inside.

"How much are you going to take?" she cried to the man who was overseeing the operation.

Everything, she was told, belonged to Baggotts of Birmingham. For the first time ever, she made her way over to their shop across the Square and asked to see Mr. Baggott. She waited for an hour outside his office.

"I have nowhere to go!" she said to him. "And your people are taking everything!"

He was a blustering sort of man who did not meet her eye.

"Look Miss." he said, "You agreed to this. You signed the forms. It's all legal. It happens all the time. Go to London. Lots of shops there. You'll get employment."

Her meeting had lasted less than a minute.

That night, she slept on the cold floor. She had one more option before she left for London. Ophelia Groves might take pity on her and help her.

CHAPTER TWENTY-FOUR

The morning brought a torrential rain to Earlsbury, accompanied by a howling gale that stripped any remaining foliage from the trees. Brown, yellow and rust-coloured leaves churned and swirled in the rapid flow of the gutters, here and there blocking drains, causing dirty floodwaters to engulf the streets.

Emma made her way to Villiers Street, getting drenched, her cloak and gown sodden to her calves. Dripping with rain, she knocked on the Groves' door. The servant opened it. She asked for Miss Groves.

"She isn't 'ere, Miss. She's away visiting."

"Who is it, Gracie?" Mrs. Groves came into the hallway. "Emma!" she cried, looking up. "What do you want?"

Emma felt the familiar discomfort in her presence. She'd last seen her at the funeral, where she had come up and sympathised with her before disappearing quickly again into the crowds.

"I'm sorry to disturb you, Mrs. Groves. I am badly, very badly in need of assistance." Emma was mumbling, she knew. Drips of rain ran down her face. She leaned forward, expecting to be invited in from the unforgiving torrent. No invitation was forthcoming, so she stepped into the hall, still carrying her box. Puddles formed at her feet. Mrs. Groves seemed displeased at her liberty. Gracie shut the door.

"How may I be of assistance?" she asked coldly, her eyes on the cuff of her pagoda sleeve as she smoothed an imaginary crumple.

"You must know, that our shop was taken over by Baggotts, and that I am left with almost nothing, and no home."

"Your aunt was very unwise. I am sorry for it. She should have sold out long ago. She did not stand a chance, foolish woman, not that I want to speak ill of the dead, but she should have known better."

Emma bit her lip to stop a retort.

"Emma, I hope you did not come here with the intention of lodging with us."

"I have nowhere to turn."

"Well you cannot stay here. This is a small house, and we are a large family. People who are in need as you are, usually make their way to the Union Workhouse."

"The Workhouse!"

"But I have just thought of something better, Emma." She brightened. "Go and try your fortunes in London. With your experience of shop-work, you will find employment there. There is a train in about an hour. Here, wait a moment - "she disappeared for a few minutes into the parlour, and returned with something in her hand. "- there, five shillings. On your way with you, and good luck."

Somehow Emma was bundled out into the street again, and the door was firmly shut. Emma was mortified! To have had money shoved into her palm, and dismissed like that! It was humiliating!

It was not money she wanted; but kindness.

Mrs. Groves went back to her parlour. She hoped it was five shillings well spent. She had only given it to her so that it would extend her stay in London until she found a position. It might not be easy. She was such a gauche country girl, was Emma!

There was a loud knock on the door again. Gracie went to answer it; Mrs. Groves caught Emma's voice, and it banged shut.

"What is it, Gracie?"

"It's Miss Mayfield, Ma'am. She said to return this." Gracie dropped the money onto a silver tray and offered it to her mistress.

"Ungrateful girl!" But Mrs. Groves was not unhappy. Andrew could come home for Christmas, without any fear of meeting her!

CHAPTER TWENTY-FIVE

Sitting in the train, Emma began to feel very cold. She was wet through. Her boots leaked, and her stockings were wet. Her cloak, a wool worsted, had been no barrier to the rain. Her hair was dripping, and she felt rivulets of cold water down her back. She began to shiver.

She thought the journey to Paddington would never end, and she got out and set off to find a place to stay and a bowl of soup. It was raining hard here as well. The big city frightened her, she'd never been outside Earlsbury before except to go to Banbury and Oxford, and she was sure some great evil would befall her in these endless, unfamiliar streets where every face was a strange one. A fine coach and four went by, splashing her from head to toe with muddy brown water.

Was there no kind face? Was there nobody to see that she was in need of assistance or guidance?

She spotted a policeman. Surely he would help her! The bobby in Earlsbury was a friendly chap and had often chatted with Aunt in the shop.

"Excuse me," she began. "Please can you tell me sir, where I might find a place to stay?" This policeman was a man of middle age, with keen, wise eyes that took her in immediately.

"Just up from the country, are you, Miss?"

"Yes."

"I'd be careful then if I was you. London can be a bad place. Some would rob you as soon as look at you. A young woman like yourself is a target for thieves and worse than thieves. Keep your money in two places on your person so that if you're robbed, you'll still 'ave some left. Now as for a place to stay, I know of one that might suit, down the street there – turn second left, then first right, and go to the fourth door on the right."

She thanked him, very relieved on the one hand, on the other, very fearful at his words.

She knocked upon the door, but the lodging house was full. She asked to be recommended to another, and after that, another – until she had knocked on seven doors and was shivering from head to toe. Every house was in a poorer street than the last one. Now she was in a very dirty, slum area. Few were out in the rain, but she saw faces inside soiled, cracked windows. Stepping into the gutter to cross the street, a large rat swam past her feet. She drew back in horror.

At last, she was accepted into a dingy house where at least a fire burned in the parlour, if you could call the dreary room with peeling paint and rickety chairs a parlour. She was shivering violently. The landlady showed her upstairs to a gloomy, chilly dormitory, where ticking on the floor served as beds. Some women were sleeping there.

"Where can I get some food?" she begged the landlady, who did not look at all clean, tidy or caring.

"You 'ave to supply yer own vittles, but I'll see if I 'ave some broth and bread, It'll cost you a shilling. I'll bring it to the parlour."

After changing into dry clothes, and hanging up her wet ones across a rope in the dormitory, she went downstairs. The broth was greasy and tasteless, the bread had mould. She pushed it away from her and went upstairs again, falling on her mattress. She had a fever, and shook violently. She closed her eyes and slept, in spite of the city noises outside.

CHAPTER TWENTY-SIX

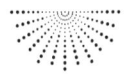

She awoke with her throat on fire.

It was nighttime. A few candles lit up the long room. The girls were up and about. She caught threads of their conversation before she opened her eyes.

"Where are you 'eaded tonight, Janice?"

"Ten Bells, where else?"

"Your sailor boy again, then?"

"No! I'll do better'n that, a lot better. A sea-captain at least, Enid. With a parrot on 'is shoulder!"

The girls laughed. The conversation went on in this vein, and Emma wondered if she had come to a house of ill-repute.

"Who is the newcomer, then?"

She opened her eyes, to see several pairs of eyes turned in her direction. She opened her mouth to speak, but no sound came.

"She's not in a talking mood, so leave 'er."

"Up from the country, poor chit of a girl. Like me fifteen years ago – wish I'd never left."

Dressed in gaudy hats and shawls, and gowns that showed too much ankle, they left the dormitory. She felt a raging thirst come upon her, and struggled to her feet. They'd left a candle lighting, and she caught sight of a jug and a cup on a table. She took a long drink, and fell back asleep. When she woke again in the morning, she was covered in itchy spots and knew that the mattress was infested. She'd have to leave here today, no matter what! The women were back, and some had gone to bed, others sat around chatting. She kept her eyes shut, not wishing to be spoken to, and fell asleep again. Stirring briefly at one stage, a woman with yellow hair brought her a drink of water, felt her forehead, and told her she needed a doctor. Emma shook her head. Doctors cost money, as did medicine. She'd get over it on her own.

"Are you very ill, Miss?" asked a woman she did not remember seeing before, who came into the room that evening when nobody was about. She was older than the other girls. She peered down at Emma by the light of a candle she carried. She looked tidy and respectable, with bright, alert eyes, a poke bonnet and a fringed shawl.

"I'm Mrs. Benson, an acquaintance of Mrs. Tyrell, the landlady. She calls me in if she 'as any girl in need of care or friendship, and you are in need of both, by the looks of you. Mrs. Tyrell, rough an' ready as she is, took pity on you, and sent me a message today. You see I am employed in a lodging house, a place of refuge for girls such as you, new to London. My brother owns it, and 'is wife is cook. London is a tough place to get yourself settled."

Mrs. Benson began to look after her; sponging her forehead, helping her to sit up and making her drink a cup of water.

"I used to nurse sick people – still do, now and then. Now, will you come tomorrow to *The Refuge for Young Women Newly-Arrived*? There's no charge, we do it for Charity. He's a good man, my brother Richard. He and his wife spends themselves for their poor girls. You'll be looked after there, and 'ave a room to yourself. All our girls 'ave their own rooms."

"It's so kind of you to suggest it." Emma felt a little apprehension, but dismissed it. She did not know this woman at all, but she was prepared to be kind to her, and Emma needed kindness more than anything else. "It's good to know that there are people who will help others in need."

"Of course, Emma. What are we all here for, only to 'elp and assist each other? We can 'elp you find a situation too. We find places for all our girls, and so 'appy they are too!"

"When I'm better, I hope to get a position in a shop, for I grew up in a shop, and I know the trade well."

"Do you indeed! A shop! That sounds fancy enough."

Mrs. Benson helped her to wash and dress the following day, and after paying Mrs. Tyrell three shillings and threepence for her bed and board, Emma walked outside to a waiting cart. A big, surly man with a beaky nose helped her up on the back, set her box beside her and they set off through a warren of streets, one more narrow than another, until they reached a decrepit house by London Docks. Was this the Refuge? There was no sign on it. Emma was not at all encouraged, but Mrs. Benson was so kind, and smothered her with attention, that she told herself she had no call to be nervous. By now, she'd confided many of her troubles to the older woman, and Mrs. Benson knew she was utterly alone in the world.

CHAPTER TWENTY-SEVEN

She climbed three flights of stairs. The room was very small and bare, with a narrow bed, a wardrobe and a table. The wallpaper had once been elegant but great strips were now missing, revealing chipped plaster underneath. The window was covered with thin red curtains. A mat lay on the floorboards and a small fire burned in the grate.

"Dorothy!" said Mrs. Benson sharply to a young servant who appeared. "Why is the fire so poor? Build it up, stupid girl!" The girl looked grim as she bent to pile coal on the grate, causing a good blaze.

Emma was soon asleep after the exertions of the morning. As usual, she placed her purse underneath her pillow. Remembering the policeman's advice, she kept her money in two places. What was not in her purse was in a drawer underneath her handkerchiefs.

She wondered how long it was before she would meet the others; she supposed after she was better, she would be allowed downstairs for meals. She looked forward to meeting new friends. Were they all new to London?

For three days and nights, she kept to her room. Mrs. Benson visited morning and evening and Dorothy brought her meals and emptied the chamber pot. Emma would have liked a little conversation, but Dorothy was not the talkative kind. She was taciturn and never smiled.

Opening the curtains on the third day, for she felt better, she saw it looked out on a junkyard and beyond that, an endless vista of roofs and chimneys. This part of London had no appeal for her, indeed she had not seen any part she liked yet!

CHAPTER TWENTY-EIGHT

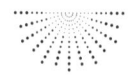

That night, she awoke to a desperate sobbing coming from one of the other rooms. Unable to bear it, she went to her door and turned the knob. But her door was locked. Locked in for the night! She was surprised. Why had she not heard Mrs. Benson lock it as she left? She must have done so very quietly indeed!

The following morning, she asked Mrs. Benson about her locked door.

"That's for your own safety," she was told. "There are all kinds of dreadful people here in the Docklands, foreign sailors for instance."

"But why can't I lock it myself then, from the inside?"

Mrs. Benson made no reply for a moment.

"I do not like to say this," she said then. "But occasionally, we 'ave a girl here who invites men in. That's why we lock the doors from the outside. We must maintain the morals of our Refuge."

Emma was silent.

"I heard a girl sobbing last night." she said, "It was so dreadful. I thought her heart was breaking."

"She 'ad a death in the family." said Mrs. Benson. "Now, have you 'ad enough porridge? I'm glad you're eating again. You're getting better at last."

"I thought I might get up today and go downstairs –"

"Oh no, far too soon! Oh, by the by," she said then, casually. "You'd better give me your money, and I'll put it under lock and key for you."

"I think I'd prefer to keep it with me." said Emma. A lifetime in trade had made her prudent, and she knew she was well able to look after it herself.

"Well Emma, it's the policy here, not to allow any guest to keep money in their rooms, because if it's stolen, it creates a great embarrassment to everybody. There are girls 'ere who are light-fingered."

"I have it with me at all times." Emma reassured her. "I am very well able to look after my money."

"All the same, it's policy. My brother makes the rules, and he's coming back today from a voyage. Why. Emma, you look as if you don't trust me! Me, who 'as looked after you like a mother for days on end! That's 'urtful, that is."

Emma felt guilt flood her. Mrs. Benson had looked after her like a mother, had seen to her every need, been so kind!

Mrs. Benson began to walk sadly toward the door.

"All right, Mrs. Benson. I didn't mean to hurt you, it's just that a policeman told me to trust nobody."

"Well 'e was right there, this city is full of crooks! But am I a crook? Have I given you any cause to think me a crook?"

"No, Mrs. Benson, you've been very kind to me." Emma felt ashamed.

Emma handed over her purse.

"Thank you, Emma." Mrs. Benson was still affronted as she took it and walked from the room.

"Should we not count it together?" Emma asked her.

"Of course we should." Mrs. Benson returned, spilled the money out on the counterpane, and they agreed it was five pounds, eleven shillings and twopence. Emma asked for a receipt and Mrs. Benson returned with one.

Emma settled back to a long day of doing nothing except sleeping and thinking. There were a few old books in a drawer but nothing that held her interest.

CHAPTER TWENTY-NINE

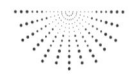

E mma woke in the dead of night to the sounds of screams and loud knocking coming from a nearby room. It sent chills through her.

The woman's screams tore the dark, cold night; the bangs on the door seemed to shake the house.

"Let me out! Let me out! You can't hold me here!" There was a commotion on the stairs, doors banged, shouts, more screams, muffled now – and silence followed. But it was a haunting silence. It hung heavy on the house. Emma began to be afraid.

"I will leave here tomorrow," she said to herself, as she snuggled under the blankets, cold in spite of their warmth. At first light, she got up and went to the wardrobe, pulling the door open.

Her clothes were gone.

She was thoroughly frightened now, but decided not to allow Mrs. Benson to see it. She was very cordial to her upon her morning visit, when her door was unlocked for the day. But she'd get something out of Dorothy when she brought breakfast. She was used to talking to people and knew how to get information without seeming to ask for it.

"Who was crying during the night, Dorothy? I hope it wasn't you."

"Oh no, Miss! Not me!"

"Then who was it? It made me feel very frightened!"

Dorothy was silent.

"It must have been one of the other girls, maybe a bad dream, do you think it was a bad dream?"

"Maybe, Miss."

"But you're not sure…I think, Dorothy, that the girl felt she was a prisoner here, but why would she feel that?"

Again, no reply.

"She is a prisoner, isn't she? And I am too?"

Dorothy did not reply.

Emma was growing afraid. But still, the servant said nothing.

"Dorothy, please tell me the truth about the happenings here." Emma opened her hand. In it, lay a shiny half-guinea, one of the coins she had carefully hidden. Thank God for that wise old policeman! Dorothy looked at it, her eyes fixed upon it. Emma closed her fist again.

"If I gave you this, what would you do with it, Dorothy?"

"I'd run away and go 'ome to Yorkshire, Miss, to my mother. I was very stupid comin' 'ere. They pays me nothing. They withheld a years wages from me now."

"If you help me, I will help you. But you must tell me what's going on."

Dorothy bent to clean the ashes out of the fireplace. She spoke in a whisper as she scraped the iron grate.

"The girls they bring 'ere, always new to London. Some are sickening. They nurse them back to health and then put them on a ship."

Emma was horrified. "A ship! To where?"

"I don't rightly know, Miss. I heard West Indies, or Africa, or Constant-iple. Something like that. A long ways away. They never can come back."

"How long do they stay here, before they are put on a ship?" Emma's mouth was dry.

"Usually after Mr. Spaulding puts in from Bristol, he sails off again within a week or so with the new girls. He brings them as far as there and then 'ands 'em over to a seagoing vessel. He's back today and he'll be up to see you, I expect."

Emma received this news with horror. She instinctively covered her bosom with her hands.

"But don't worry, Miss. Them that wants the girls, don't want any used goods."

"Dorothy, please help me to get out of here. I beg you. We can help each other!" Trembling, she put the coin in her hand and closed her fist around it. "I have more, more than enough to get you back to Yorkshire. Don't tell on me, please! We'll leave this house together!"

CHAPTER THIRTY

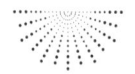

Oxford looked splendid even in winter, Andrew thought, as he gathered his books and left for his lodgings near Christ Church. At this time of year, the trees were bare, and the buildings stood magnificent in their own glory without receiving any help from nature. He loved the town, its high, grave buildings, spires, domes and towers. His walks in winter were crisp and invigorating. He had settled in very well in the past year and his pleasant and sincere personality had ensured that he had made many good friends.

He had put Earlsbury, and Emma out of his head. The world was a very big place, and Earlsbury so small! His society there had been very limiting. Though he retained tender feelings for his first love, he knew that a future with her could not be. His mother had written some time ago that she was walking out with a coachmaker's apprentice who would be a good match for her. He had felt regretful at the time, as if some happiness had passed him by, but realised that it was for the best. On their last meeting, he had thought of marriage, and almost declared himself to her! Thank Heaven he had not done that.

He had not been in Earlsbury for almost a year now. His mother had contrived to keep him away at Easter, and for the summer they had all repaired to Lake Geneva, a holiday that had almost bankrupted the family.

A letter awaited him in his room.

Dear Andrew, I do hope you will join us at Christmas, but if you are invited anywhere of note, please be at liberty to accept that invitation. We are well here. Perhaps you know that Mayfields Shop is shut up after the death of poor Mrs. Mayfield. Emma has set off to seek her fortune in London. She was very glad to leave this little place I am sure, there is nothing for her here, with her unfortunate birth always to her disadvantage. She came to me to say goodbye and looked very happy. I wished her very well indeed. She can blend into London with others of her level, and will do very well I am sure.

Andrew put his coat back on and put the letter in his pocket. He strode past the old grey buildings, along the pathways, and into to the woods, to be alone. There was a frost coming on and it was getting chilly and darkness fell before he knew it. The moon rose. He halted on a bridge over the Cherwell, his elbows on the wooden supports, hearing rather than seeing the churning waters below. His thoughts and feelings were a maelstrom of confusion and anger.

Mrs. Mayfield had died – nobody had told him until now. He guessed that his sisters had been forbidden to write of it in their letters. And Emma had jauntily set off for London – what a ridiculous notion, what a lie! He knew Emma! And more than that, he knew the financial affairs of the Mayfield Emporium. Deeply in debt, a debt that Mrs. Mayfield had hoped to turn around somehow. But in the time left to her, it would not at all have been possible! She had died unexpectedly – leaving Emma alone with a huge debt – Andrew knew that Emma would never have been able to stand up to those who would have come after her. He felt nauseated. And where was she now? What of the coachmaker? He was not in the picture or his mother would have mentioned it – been very happy to have placed her in an engagement, farther away from him.

"What's up, chap?" asked Lord Edison, after he returned to the house. "I was afraid you had bad news. Are they all well, your family?"

"Yes, all well."

"Good! Will you think about a Christmas visit to Edison Hall then, if they don't need you? Annabel has particularly asked me if you should be at liberty to join us for the Festivities? My sisters and brothers have planned all sorts of fun and games and they have strongly hinted at a Theatrical, in which, Groves, you will be expected to take the romantic lead opposite Annabel, who will insist on being the leading lady."

Andrew gazed out the window at the lights twinkling in the towers and houses, at the spires and the moon shining above.

The Edison family often visited their son and brother, and he had been invited with them upon picnics and luncheons. They were a bright, happy bunch. He was fond of Miss Edison, she was pretty, and kind. She also liked him, very much. He had in the last few months, after Michaelmas when they had taken a long walk together, felt that they could be happy together, and his lack of means did not seem to disturb her, or her parents. But the letter had banished all feeling for Miss Edison. His love for Emma rekindled with the passion that only a first love can bring. Emma was in need, and he burned to find her.

He knew he had to return to Earlsbury for Christmas. He had to find out, in detail, all that had happened to Mayfield Emporium and more importantly, had to find any clue that would lead him to Emma.

"My family expect me for Christmas," he said, turning around. "I shall have to postpone the pleasure of visiting your family until another time. Please convey to them my deepest regrets."

"Oh." Something in his tone made Edison understand that his sister was about to suffer a broken heart. Did Groves have a sweetheart in Earlsbury? But he had never let on anything about another girl! He had seen though, once, in his room, a sketch of a dark-haired young woman with wide expressive eyes. It had been a portrait of the girl's heart as much as of her face and hair, drawn with thought and care. He wished he had asked him about the portrait at the time.

CHAPTER THIRTY-ONE

There was commotion in the *Refuge for Young Women Recently Arrived.* Mrs. Benson arrived up with a tray of bread and butter and tea around six-o-clock.

"That wench Dorothy," she said. "'as upped and left. Just like that."

"Oh no," said Emma, the words dying on her lips lest they give away her feelings. A sensation of dread and disbelief came over her. The loss of hope crept into her bones; a curtain dropped over her future, she began to be terrified but tried not to show it.

"It's not all that bad, we'll get another," snapped Mrs. Benson. "But now I'm expected to do the serving, and I've enough to do!"

When she was alone, she flung herself on her bed, banging her fists upon the pillow.

How could she have been so stupid? A half-guinea would take a person to Yorkshire and back ten times!

At least she was not suspected of having any part in it. She'd had a visitor during the day, the said Mr. Spaulding, brought to the room by his wife. He had stared at her with vulgar curiousity. Knowing what his business was, she'd received him coldly and without the gratitude expected of her. Then he had muttered that he was glad she was recovering, and he knew a good shop in Mayfair who were looking for lady assistants. She'd shaken a fist after him after he had left, telling him silently that she would be gone tomorrow or the next day, and he could sing for his supper.

But now Dorothy had bolted with the half-guinea; by now, she was probably drinking tea in her mother's kitchen in Leeds!

'Emma, how could you have been so stupid? Why did you not just give her a shilling, and the promise of more? Oh Aunt, if you could see me now, you would say I was the stupidest girl in England! What am I going to do? I will have to make a run for it, overcome Mrs. Benson when

she comes in to get the tea-tray – no – tomorrow morning – the breakfast tray – how do I do it? I shall have to steal her clothes, oh if only I could talk to the other girls. I wonder if I knocked upon the wall, would anybody answer me. Could we perhaps establish some communication, so that we could form a plan?

Could I shout out the window? Would Mrs. Benson or the Spauldings hear me? What if all of us girls could somehow communicate with each other and we could shout all at the same time. Oh Emma, why were you so stupid?

'This could be the end of everything. I wish I could get a message to Andrew, even if he has forgotten me, he would not stand by!'

Mrs. Benson, accompanied by Mrs. Spaulding, a stout woman in a long white apron and frilled cap, came back in for the tea-tray.

"You haven't eaten anything," she accused. "You have to eat."

"Why is that? To build me up for the voyage?"

"You know! Who told you?"

"I did not have to ask anybody if I was a prisoner here. The locked door, my clothes gone, my money taken. What do you plan to do with me?"

Mrs. Benson said nothing, but was startled by a loud banging on the door.

"Open up! Police!"

CHAPTER THIRTY-TWO

It had happened very quickly. The police had broken down the door, Mrs. Benson and Mrs. Spaulding had run to the attics. The girls – seven in all – had been freed. Shy of the men, they'd raided the rooms until they'd found their clothes, before they convened in the parlour where the policemen waited to take their statements. The two women had been found hiding under beds and carted off, shouting loudly.

Dorothy sauntered in. She had conducted the police there, and afraid to come in until she saw that the raid had been successful, had waited until now to make her presence known.

"You see, Miss Emma. Why should only you and I go free, when I could get us all free?"

"Oh Dorothy, you are a wonder! When I heard you'd left, I thought you'd gone off up to Yorkshire!"

"Why din't you go to the police long afore now?" demanded a girl named Sophie, with scorn. "You coulda gone anytime!"

"I wor a prisoner too, worn't I? But with money, I wor able to bribe Pelican. I told 'im I 'ad to go out on an urgent errand. It took me a full hour to find someone who would listen to a poor misery like me, and get police! Pelican's up 'alf-a-guinea, and 'es drinkin' it, I'll bet, and the police will want "im too."

"*The Pelican?*" asked Darlene, a girl from the West Country.

"The man with the hookey nose." said Molly, from Dublin. "But what of Mr. Spaulding? He wasn't here and they'll never find him. But what are we to do now?"

"I still 'ave to get ter *Yorkshire*," said Dorothy with meaning, looking at Emma.

"Of course!" Emma brought her aside and gave her two guineas; Dorothy had indeed produced a master stroke. She was sorry she couldn't give her more – even if she had a thousand gold sovereigns it would be impossible to repay Dorothy! Dorothy looked very happy however with her two guineas.

"You'll all be required to give evidence at the Trial," said the Constable, "so leave your addresses."

He wondered why some of them laughed.

CHAPTER THIRTY-THREE

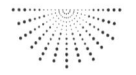

Mr. Spaulding was furious. All Hell had broken loose while he had been out negotiating a contract with the owners of a ship who would take this lot as far as Cairo. He had turned the corner in time to see his wife and sister borne off in the grip of several constables, and had fled.

How had this happened? He had control over all of his staff, and the loyalty of his wife and sister were unquestionable. He went to The Top Mast, found his strong man Harvey there, soused. He was too short a man to beat up The Pelican, but he had him removed to another house he owned where he wouldn't be able to talk to anybody. The Pelican was going to have a do a job for him though. He was going to have to find and follow these seven girls and make sure that none of them would testify in court. It wouldn't be very hard – they had no money. None of them had anything, except that girl who had surrendered five pounds. Who was she? A shop girl? He'd find her first because she didn't like him, and was probably the sharpest and most likely to pursue justice.

CHAPTER THIRTY-FOUR

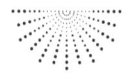

The girls were referred to Lady Kinnaird's home for migrant and displaced girls which she had founded in Charlotte Street. But they only stayed there for a short time. Three of the girls were anxious to return to their homes in the country; they were immediately provided with their fares. Positions in domestic service were found for three. One girl was a hat-maker and a situation in a millinery was found for her. The last was Emma, and confident that she would be taken on in any London shop that would give her a chance, she set out one day to search. But after three days of enquiry in shops large and small, she returned every day to the North London Refuge discouraged. She had learned three things:

Most shops employed men because respectable shops were suspicious of female assistants.

Those department stores who employed women in their Ladies departments looked down their noses and required that she have the skills of a lady's maid, measuring, making adjustments, and flattering her rich customers.

Her accounting skills were not an asset, for male clerks handled everything monetary.

The days were getting cold and dark, the Home was full; at least she had friends there now. Every girl was trying to find her way in the world, and they shared advice and experiences. Christmas was almost upon them; shop windows were filling up with bright decorations and toys galore. She kept up her search, surely, in this busy time, somebody would take her on, if only to be generous in the spirit of the Season!

CHAPTER THIRTY-FIVE

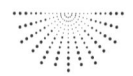

It did not take long for Mr. Spaulding to find out where the women had been taken. A bribe to an associate he had with contacts in the Metropolitan Police had produced the required result. He and Harvey took a closed carriage up toward Fitzroy Square two days before Christmas and waited a little way down Charlotte Street.

Emma was returning after another gloomy, fruitless quest, her eyes down, thinking that Christmas or no, shops were not willing to take a chance of a young woman assistant, not even as a temporary hand. Raising her head, she noticed the carriage. She recognised the figure on the box – *the Pelican*! She drew back into the shadows, terrified that she had been seen. Her fears were confirmed when the horses started a trot in her direction. She turned and ran away as fast as she could. She did not even know where she was going.

CHAPTER THIRTY-SIX

Mrs. Groves greeted her oldest son with a warm embrace. Everything was going well for her, and she was only a little upset that Andrew did not seem to be in the Christmas spirit. He was restless and cross and barely noticed the decorations his young sister and brother had been making.

"What's the news about the Mayfields?" he asked abruptly, after he had doffed his coat and was looking about the house after his long absence.

"Mayfields!" exclaimed his mother. "There is no news about Mayfields. I told you they went out of business."

"They were taken over by Baggotts of Birmingham," said his father.

"I hope Emma got her annuity?"

"Indeed, I do not know, Andrew. It wasn't any of our business to get involved in the matter."

"She's not seventeen, Mother and ignorant of the ways of the world."

"How are the Edisons, Andrew?" said his mother, pointedly changing the subject. "Have they invited you to spend any part of the Christmas holidays at their country home?"

"Oh, all of it actually, but I declined."

"I thought you liked Miss Edison," teased Ophelia. "You wrote to me that she had an uncommonly refined and sweet disposition."

Andrew got up suddenly and walked about the room.

"I'm going out," he said abruptly.

"What did I say?" Ophelia cried.

"Nothing. In fact, if you'd like to come for a walk, Philly, I'd appreciate it."

Brother and sister walked to the busy Square, where the lights shone brightly in Baggotts windows. Children, bundled up in coats and hats, jumped up and down with glee, watching a row of toy soldiers that by some mechanical trick revolved around its base. A smell of gingerbread came from the bakery. A little crowd surrounded a group from St. Michael's Church singing *'Ding Dong Merrily on High'* with much ringing of handbells.

Opposite Baggotts, what had been Mayfields shop was a dark, lonely building, the windows boarded up, and tiles missing from the roof from a recent storm.

"I have to ask you, Philly, if I were to find Emma and make her my wife, if she was willing that is – would you accept her, or, would you, like Mother, reject her because of the circumstances of her birth?"

"I only would want what would make you happiest," Ophelia said. "I've always found Emma to be a pleasant, sweet girl, and if she were to become my sister, I would have no objection at all."

"Thank you, Philly. I wouldn't want to make her part of a family that rejected her."

"Do you know where she is then?" asked Ophelia.

He dug his hands in his pockets and looked across at the forlorn building.

"No, I have no idea. Tomorrow, I shall go and see Mr. Williams, the attorney who handled the Mayfield affairs. I hope she left an address, or gave some clue as to where she was going."

"Something for the poor, sir!" asked a boy who was collecting for the carol singers.

"Oh, yes. Of course." He dropped in a shilling. Thought he felt very gloomy about Emma, and worried about her, it was still Christmas, a time of Hope, and he had to cling to that. It wasn't good to feel any hopelessness at this time of year.

CHAPTER THIRTY-SEVEN

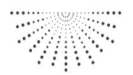

Emma kept running until she almost fell from exhaustion. She knew they followed her for a time, she heard the galloping and the angry shouts from people on foot as the carriage rushed through the streets thronged with Christmas shoppers. She attracted curious stares as she ran. Perhaps some of these people might have helped her, but she did not stop to find out. She was terrified of Spaulding, of the Pelican, and the thought of what could happen to her. She slowed a little – where was she? She saw signs that said she was in or near Covent Garden. As soon as she came to an alley that she knew would not admit the carriage, she took it. Out of breath, she hid in a damp, smelly alcove, and peered around it to see if she was to be pursued on foot. Her thoughts crowded her.

In an alley, if they caught up with her, she could be in more danger than on the streets. And tomorrow was her birthday! Was she not to see seventeen? Would her lifeless body, found in the dawn of Christmas Eve, be taken to some horrid, chilly morgue while a policeman wondered how to find out who she was? For she was sure that no trace of her identity would be left upon her to point to her killers.

Then she would be buried in a pauper's grave and forgotten. Nobody would miss her or mourn her.

Perhaps she should just allow them to kill her, and end her misery! *Stop these thoughts*, she said to herself.

She was not being pursued now, so she came out of the alcove, and walked down the alley – to what? To where? Tears blurred her eyes and she did not see the steps until she was tumbling.

She cried out, trying to stop her fall, but was helpless until she rolled to the bottom.

"Dear, dear, what's this?" the voice of an old woman was in her ear, and she felt herself being patted gently on the arm." Are you hurt, luv? Can you get up?" A small candle was set on a ledge.

Emma got herself slowly to her feet, she felt bruised all over and was shaking from head to foot.

"You'd best come inside," said the old woman, who had soft brown eyes, and snow-white hair visible under her mob-cap. "You've had a nasty shock."

'Inside' was a basement room, ill-lit but warm from a smoky fire. There was an aroma of something tasty.

"Beef broth, Miss." The old lady pushed a bowl into her hands. "Drink it up."

"But – it's yours!" Emma objected. "This is your supper!"

"Bless you, dear child. How kind you are. I have all I need. Drink up, then you can tell me why you fell down my steps."

"I was running from people who want me killed."

If the old lady thought that this was an odd thing for somebody to say she did not give any sign to Emma, but said "Go on," in a most encouraging tone, as she shook a spoon of tea-leaves into a whistling kettle on the fire.

"I'd best start at the beginning," Emma said. "I was an unwanted child, a child abandoned in a churchyard…" she talked for a long time. As she spoke, she became aware that the woman seated in front of her, was sitting under an odd sort of picture in a frame. She couldn't make it out, and she did not know why it held her attention - it was almost familiar.

CHAPTER THIRTY-EIGHT

"Your story is indeed tragic," said the old woman. "But it is not an unusual one. I know a child who was conceived as you must have been, out of wedlock. A poor child who, before he was weaned, had deadly enemies. People wanted him killed."

"That's dreadful indeed." said Emma. "I hope they didn't succeed!"

"No. He grew up in safety." The woman's eyes had a tear.

"Was he – was he your child?" asked Emma, gulping down her tea, which had gone cold because she had talked for so long.

"No, not my child. But he was a gift to the world. You, too, are a gift to the world."

"I'm a gift to the world?" Emma was astonished. "I've questioned all my life if I was meant to be here. Aunt Jane, of course, used to say I was a blessing to her. But now that she's dead, how could I be a blessing to anybody else? Nobody wants me. Even –"

"Never think that, Emma. You were created for a purpose. I'm sure you know now, what child it is of whom I spoke. Do you?"

"It must be Jesus," said Emma.

There was a little silence. Emma thought that the old woman looked tired, and it struck her that she had kept her up. She got up to go. She still felt shocked and bruised all over.

"Where will you go?" asked the old woman. "I haven't much here, but you can sleep on that little trundle bed by the fire."

Emma looked about.

"Where do you sleep, Mrs - em " she did not know what the woman's name was, and she had not volunteered it.

"I don't sleep at this time." said the old woman. "The bed is yours."

Emma was puzzled, but grateful. She fell asleep soon afterwards curled up under a blanket. The last thought in her head was that she should go home for Christmas Eve, though she had no home now in Earlsbury. Of course! How had she not thought of it! She would wait in the churchyard as she had the year before, and this time, instead of throwing a tantrum, reveal her desperate circumstances and beg for help. They, whoever they were, could not – would not – refuse help to her! They had *some* feeling for her. She would tell the old woman in the morning of her plans.

When she woke, it was past dawn. The woman was nowhere to be seen. Lighting the stub of a candle, Emma looked about her. She seemed to be in the basement of an old shop. She saw a great deal of merchandise, old and gathering dust, such as they had stocked at Mayfields. Everything was covered in dust and cobwebs. The fire looked as if it had not been lit for a long time. The ashes were stone cold.

Where was the old lady? And the pot, and the bowl? It was very odd indeed! As she turned to leave, something caught her eye. The framed picture on the wall. She went and examined it more closely. It was a tangle of coloured threads. Something flashed into her mind – her grandmother's tale of the tapestry. She took down the picture and turned it around in her hands. But as it was in a frame, the other side was covered in backing. She hung it back on the wall, thoughtfully.

She emerged onto the alley, rubbing her eyes in the light. She was not going to go back to Charlotte Street, she was not safe there anymore. She would catch a train for Earlsbury, but first, she wished to go back to the basement to leave a Christmas gift for the old woman who had been so kind to her. She thought that a box of linen handkerchiefs would be nice for her, and chose some from a little shop in Floral Street, spending nearly all of her money on them, and asking for a position into the bargain, only to be turned down by the courteous manager with the familiar reply *'I am sorry, Miss, we do not employ ladies.'*

She retraced her steps briskly and went down the alley she was sure she had taken the night before, but no steps, nor any basement, was to be found. She tried several alleys to the left and right, and thoroughly perplexed now, gave up. It was late, and she had to hurry now, to get to Earlsbury before dark.

She made her way to Paddington, to find to her dismay that the trains were not running on Christmas Eve. But she was determined, and set off for the London-Oxford Road, resolved to find a stagecoach going in that direction.

CHAPTER THIRTY-NINE

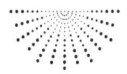

"It's Christmas Eve, sir. Mr. Williams is on holiday today." The butler frowned.

"This is a matter of great urgency," Andrew said. "I must see him."

"I will tell him, sir," said the butler, with the attitude of bestowing an extraordinary favour.

Andrew waited impatiently on the doorstep of the Georgian house until the butler re-appeared and allowed him in. He was shown into a cold drawing room.

"Mr. Groves," said Mr. Williams who appeared in his dressing-gown. "You must excuse my not being dressed. I was not expecting any business today – and at this hour too – just after eight o'clock! I understand that there is some urgency about your visit?" He motioned to him to sit down.

"I have come about Miss Mayfield." Andrew said.

"Miss Mayfield?" Mr. Williams seemed surprised. "What of her? She has come to no harm, I hope?"

"I was hoping that you could tell me that. I wish to know what became of her."

"You are the first person to make any enquiry..." Mr. Williams appeared to be at a loss as to what to say.

Andrew looked impatient. It was Christmas Eve and everybody was supposed to be merry and bright, but he could not feel it.

"Do you have her forwarding address?"

"She did not leave any."

"What? To where are her communications sent? Her annuity, for instance?"

There was a pause.

"What annuity?" Mr. Williams sat up.

"I know that her aunt arranged an annuity of thirty pounds a year, some time ago."

Mr. Williams coughed.

"Mr. Groves, I found no papers in her – files – to support that."

"What, man? Were they lost? And if they were, was it not with you that Mrs. Mayfield would have arranged it? Do not you remember? You were named as her Guardian until she came of age!"

"She must have made the guardianship arrangement with another person," said Mr. Williams, getting up. "I know nothing about it. Mrs. Mayfield died bankrupt and Baggotts of Birmingham bought up all of her assets, shop, house, debts, everything."

A flash of anger lit up Andrew's eyes.

"How can you say you know nothing of it, Mr. Williams? For I saw it. She invited me to be privy to all of her private papers and correspondence. You are Miss Mayfield's guardian until she comes of age or marries, whichever comes first."

Mr. Williams turned pale. His eyes narrowed.

"I admit that there was an annuity, but it was cancelled."

"Cancelled? How? Why?"

"The attorneys of Baggotts of Birmingham demanded it. They did not wish it to come from the

Estate of Mrs. Mayfield, for over decades, should she live to be seventy or eighty, it would amount to a great amount."

"It was coming from The Gault&Evans Assurance Company - ,"

"In turn guaranteed by Mayfield Emporium, which was not solvent. Baggotts of Birmingham were to take over all the obligations."

"- but it could not have been cancelled, without Miss Mayfield or her representative, which would have been you, consenting to it, and signing the necessary releases."

Mr. Williams got up abruptly.

"Miss Mayfield signed; I counter-signed and my clerk witnessed, it was all accomplished legally; I discussed it all with her and what it meant. I have all the papers should you wish to inspect them."

"How could a young woman who has not attained her majority, with no experience of the world, know what she was doing? You discussed it with her? I demand to know what you said!"

"It is Christmas, Mr. Grove, and I never as a rule discuss business at Christmas. Now, if you will excuse me – I must dress myself, and make myself ready for my wife's family who are to join us today. And this room must be got ready, I believe, for our visitors." He pulled the bell.

"You Crook!" shouted Andrew after his departing back. "You lied to my face when you said you knew nothing of the annuity, and now you have been found out! How much did Baggotts pay you? You left a young woman defenceless and penniless in the world! May God forgive you!"

CHAPTER FORTY

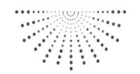

There were a great many people travelling on Christmas Eve, and it was hours later before Emma was able to find a place on a crowded coach. She squeezed in between a woman with a goose carcass in a bag which she was surreptitiously plucking as they went along, and a man who had a very severe cold. Another man wanted a window open to change the bad air; the man with the cold quarrelled with him.

She felt unwell too. The weather was freezing, and her cough, which had never fully left her, began to return as they lurched along. She felt a relapse of her condition and a fever rose. She longed to stop and find lodging and remain there for the night. She'd had nothing since the broth the evening before, but had no appetite. She felt very thirsty.

But she had to go on. Her throat was afire again. It was well after dark when she reached Earlsbury. The shops had all closed and it was too early for church-goers, so the streets were empty. After she alighted the coach the first sight that met her eyes was her old house, dark, bleak and abandoned. She looked up at it sadly.

They did not even re-open the shop, she said to herself with bitterness. *They just left it there to rot!*

She walked down the street toward St. Michael's. She felt very ill now. A hard frost was falling. The moon was up. She hurried her steps – the familiar gate creaked its familiar creak, the yews stood where they had always stood, the gravestones were the same – a few crooked among the straight. She had no lamp, so she walked with care. Uphill she went, surprised that her legs felt like lead, that instead of seventeen years old today, she seemed to be suddenly old. She reached the Mayfield grave at last and sank down. The earth was still fresh after Aunt Jane's interment. She lay down on it, cold as it was, as her legs seemed to be unable to support her any longer. She'd stay here until they arrived. She hoped with all her heart that they had not listened to her hard words of the year before! She shut her eyes, and a river of ice seemed to flood her body, causing a violent tremor. She tried to move her limbs, but could not. She dimly heard sounds of people going the road on their way to the church; a few horses went by, some greetings of *'Merry Christmas!'* reached her ears, and then, was her own name: *"Emma! Emma!"* Hands were about her, were they Angels' hands, to take her to Heaven? Was she dying, then? *Oh Lord, forgive me my sins...*

CHAPTER FORTY-ONE

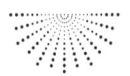

She lay on a featherbed, covered by blankets. She felt deliciously warm and cosy. Was she in Heaven, then? She turned and opened her eyes. She pulled back a little of the curtains drawn about her bed.

"Ah Miss, you're awake. Thank God!" said a woman of middle-age, with a long white apron and a cap. "You gave many people a fright."

"Where am I?" she asked, frowning, trying to gather her memories. She was in Lady Kinnaird's – no, she had come to Earlsbury, on Christmas Eve last. Since then, she had woken up briefly now and then, barely conscious of people forcing water down her throat, barely conscious of being prayed over, barely conscious of her arms being bled.

The woman drew back the bed curtains, affording her a view of her surroundings. She was in a little bedroom, very prettily furnished in white and rose pink. Tree limbs with green buds waved outside the window.

"How long have I been lying here?" she asked.

"You came here four weeks ago, Miss, and afore that, you were at the doctor's house for two. Here, you are to have some toast and tea. You haven't eaten in all that time except what we have been forcing down your throat, milk and broth, anything to keep you from death. Now, I have to send somebody with a message to your friends, and I will be back with the toast."

"Friends? Who? Where am I now?"

But the woman had disappeared, leaving her alone, and a young servant girl named Bessie came in with her breakfast.

She sat up to take her toast, and drank her tea. Falling back on the pillows, she saw that they were edged in lace. The sheets were fine linen. The counterpane was of white squares embroidered with candlewick. Who was her benefactor?

"You have visitors," announced the woman about an hour later.

Andrew Groves and his sister Ophelia stood in the little white doorway, flushed and happy.

"Andrew!" she cried happily, tears in her eyes.

He sat on the bed, taking her hands in his, speechless, his eyes moistened. Ophelia said she had been visiting her brother when the good news came, and she exulted over her recovery and after a few minutes, made an excuse to go to the kitchen.

"What happened to me, Andrew?"

"Last Christmas Eve, I found you half-dead on your aunt's grave. Frozen, almost."

"You it was who called my name, then?"

"Yes. I knew that if you came back to Earlsbury, that you would go there on Christmas Eve. Actually, you can credit my sister with that thought. Women are so much better at knowing these things! I called out for help and we carried you to Dr. Roger's house. You were unconscious and we feared you would die. I was distraught, Emma. Absolutely distraught!" He took her hands to his lips and kissed them over and over.

"After you had warmed, the doctor tried to wake you, he said that if you did not wake for nourishment, you would die. I shook you and even slapped you to wake up! Do you not remember it?"

"No! But thank you, if that's what it took!"

"You thanked me already." Andrew grinned and touched his eye area, which had a faint discolouration.

"I hit you?"

"Punched me! You should have seen it weeks ago!"

"I have no memory of that. Goodness knows what else I did or said! Was I raving?"

"You have nothing to worry about, Emma."

The nurse – whose name was Mrs. Sadlier - intervened and sent Andrew away, saying that her patient had had enough for one day.

But Emma still had not found out what she really wanted to know – where was she? Mrs. Sadlier would only say "Near Oxford."

CHAPTER FORTY-TWO

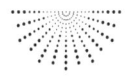

"Arthur, I beg you to reconsider. This is breaking my heart!"

"Margaret, I told you that I can't believe what your mother told you. She must have been crazed at the end. People can become incoherent on their deathbeds."

"She was not quite on her deathbed, Arthur! She lived for a week after that. And she was so sorry, so heartbroken – I hardly spoke to her until the day she died, and then I forgave her, though it made me cry for many nights. She need not have told me at all, but she could not meet God with this on her conscience."

Arthur Castleton poured himself a glass of port. His wife spoke again, pushing back her ringlets with her hand. She was not yet forty years old, and was as beautiful as when he had first laid eyes on her.

"Watkins and his wife – if only we could find them! - can testify to the truth of what I'm saying, the truth of what Mother told me."

Mr. Castleton put the glass to his lips.

"I'm not prepared to accept the girl Emma, Margaret. I think it may have been unwise to have rented the cottage at Forest Hill. But you were adamant, and I gave in. Because it was Christmas I suppose, and she was at death's door."

"You wouldn't allow me to bring her here, Arthur. And the money that Mother left me pays for the cottage and the nurse."

The door opened and a servant came in with a letter on a silver tray.

"For you, Ma'am. From Lilybell Cottage."

She took it up eagerly and tore it open.

"She is awake! She has woken up and spoken to Mr. Groves! Oh this is the happiest day of my life! Arthur, now may I go to her?"

"No, you may not. This Emma is not our Emma, Margaret! Our daughter died! And is buried in Charlbury!"

"She lived, Arthur, and she grew up as Emma Mayfield!" Mrs. Castleton flew out of the room. Her husband was an impossible man! A Professor of Natural Sciences, he could never see anything that was not in plain evidence. She went to the greenhouse to pick daffodils and hyacinth. He followed her, laying a tender hand on her shoulder.

"Margaret, I do not mean for you to become upset – can you not see my point of view? I attended the funeral of our little Emma. If she was not in the coffin, who was?"

She buried her face in his chest.

"If only we had been married at the time she was born, Arthur! Mother would not have lied to me! She thought that the child would bind me to you! And then she told me she had died and it would be better that I not see her."

"Yes, yes." her husband said, his eyes wandering to the skies. "Your mother had a very poor opinion of me, and with reason. And then when we married three months later, she became very remorseful, still did not tell you, and sent a gift every year to this

Emma, to appease her conscience. That was her tale, was it not?"

"Yes. The longer she left it, the harder and the more impossible it seemed to her to tell us."

"How did she know who took Emma in?"

"She sent Watkins to Earlsbury to find out the name of who it was he saw take the basket. Servants can find out everything from other servants and the churchyard child made local news."

"I cannot give it any credit, even now, Margaret. You must understand! I carried the little coffin myself to the grave! Are we to exhume it – it does not bear thinking about! The undertaker must be dead by now; he looked about ninety when I met him all those years ago; if there was a secret, it died with him."

"Find Watkins then and get the truth. He and his wife brought Emma to the churchyard and thereafter, Watkins left a gift every year. He lied to me when I asked him. He would not lie to you, I think."

Arthur looked doubtful again.

"I did wonder at your mother leaving them a thousand pounds," he said. "It was an exorbitant amount for a coachman and housekeeper."

"So they retired and went off somewhere. But where? If we could find them, and this time were willing to tell the truth, would you believe it then?"

"I suppose I would have to," he said.

"I want so much to see Emma, and for her to meet her brothers." Margaret said. "I want to tell her that every day, for the last seventeen years, I have thought of her, and that since Mother told me the truth, that I long to know her."

Her husband did not reply.

"I wonder if she looks like you or me," said Mrs. Castleton dreamily. "If she is like you, she may have your dark blue eyes, which I would call violet, only you object to the description."

"I certainly do object, Margaret! Dark blue, please! Leave violet for the ladies. But do not visit Miss Mayfield until I find Watkins." her husband fixed his eyes upon her and she nodded, her mood dejected again.

CHAPTER FORTY-THREE

"Where am I and what happened to me?"

Andrew told her. She was in the village of Forest Hill, near Oxford.

"Whose cottage is this?"

"A Mr. and Mrs. Castleton have rented it for you."

"Are they my parents?"

"I do not know. By the way, you were cheated by Mr. Williams. Did you know you were to get an annuity?" he told her the details.

"But it seems impossible now," she said. "He never told me anything about it, and I signed all kinds of forms, it was very confusing."

"He is your legal Guardian."

"No! Not him!"

"But I don't think he will act for you. He doesn't want attention drawn to his underhand dealings, so you're unlikely to hear from him."

"Has he called here, to enquire how I am?"

"No."

"Where do you live, Andrew?"

"I'm only fifteen minutes' walk away, through the woods."

"Does – does your mother know you visit me?"

Andrew coloured a little. "No, she doesn't."

"She told me of a Miss Edison, some time ago. And that she expected your engagement to her."

"My mother will be disappointed, then. She is determined to arrange my life!"

"Be thankful for her." Emma said.

Andrew looked at her in surprise. She was very serious. He fell silent. Was he thankful for his mother, despite all her faults? Emma thought he ought to be.

Emma began to cough. He gave her water, but it did not ease her. Finally she fell back on the pillow, her cheeks flushed from the effort, her eyes closed in fatigue.

Andrew kissed her forehead and left the cottage to walk back to his house along the woodland path. Around him, the trees and the birds had awoken to springtime, and yellow primroses peeped from the hedgerows. The joy that he had felt when Emma had awoken had now given way to another fear. Her doctor was not even sure she would fully recover. She had suffered a severe lung inflammation which had put her in danger of consumption. She still coughed – the next months would tell.

A few days later Andrew was very happy to see Emma sitting out of bed by the window, looking out upon the small colourful garden and the road beyond. It was in a quiet village, but labourers, servants, farmers' carts and even an occasional carriage passed.

"She ate a good dinner today," said the nurse. "Irish stew and dumplings."

As usual, Emma had questions, it was unsurprising, for she had plenty of time to think of them as she lay in bed or sat out.

"Did he come that night, do you know? The man who brings the gift?"

Andrew was prepared.

"After we took you to Dr. Roger's house, it was Mr. and Mrs. Castleton who came."

"They, both?"

Andrew began the story.

CHAPTER FORTY-FOUR

He was at the doctor's house, in his parlour, pacing, deadly anxious – worried that she would die upstairs. Servants ran to and fro with warmed pans and towels. He dimly heard a carriage pull up outside, but thought nothing of it. Then there was a knock at the door.

The servants were busy so Andrew went to answer it. A couple stood there. They took him for a butler, and demanded entry to see the doctor.

"I'm afraid the doctor is very busy with an emergency," he responded.

"Miss Mayfield. We want to know about Miss Mayfield." said the woman in a desperate way. She had a veil over her face.

"Come in." They followed him into the doctor's parlour.

"I'm Andrew Groves, at your service." he said to them. "A friend of Miss Mayfield's."

The woman looked quickly, almost appealingly at the man.

"We have come from Charlbury, Mr. Groves." he said. "I am Mr. Castleton and this is my wife."

"What interest do you have in Miss Mayfield?" Andrew asked them coldly. Were these her parents? He did not think much of parents who abandoned their child in a churchyard in the middle of winter.

"We came to the churchyard to attempt a meeting with her tonight," said Mrs. Castleton. "To find that she was not there, however, there were some people about, speaking of how a young woman was taken away almost – dead – and so we enquired as to the name."

"My wife believes that we are relatives." Mr. Castleton said then, in a clipped tone.

"Relatives, you say?" Andrew still felt cold toward them.

"Please – how is she?" the woman sounded desperate, her veiled eyes turned to the ceiling, to the little commotion above, to the thuds of footsteps and the short bursts of unintelligible conversation.

"I do not know. I await news, as you do." He surveyed them, trying to make them out. They were well-dressed, not poor. They sank in his estimation, if it was convenience, and not poverty, that had made them abandon their infant.

"What of Mrs. Mayfield – is she here?"

The news of her death disturbed them.

"So she is alone!" exclaimed the woman in anguish, wringing her hands. Andrew began to thaw. Perhaps he had been hasty in judgement. His heart softened toward her, but not toward him. He had a stony countenance. There was little tenderness there.

"Are you the persons who have been leaving her gifts all these years?" he asked suddenly.

The man looked down and away. The woman said:

"No. We did not know of her existence. <u>We</u> thought she was dead."

The man got up and paced the room, his lips tight.

"It was my late mother who left the gifts. She sent a servant with them," continued the woman.

"Are you her mother?" Andrew felt bold enough to ask.

"Yes." she replied, while her husband wheeled around and said:

"We do not know that we are even relatives of this unfortunate young woman."

A man's steps were heard on the stairs, and the doctor appeared in the parlour. Andrew introduced the newcomers as possible relatives of Emma Mayfield, in a tone of voice that did not exude warmth. Explanations followed, and the couple offered to take over the care of Emma as soon as she was well enough to be moved.

CHAPTER FORTY-FIVE

"And I do not know anymore than that." Andrew concluded.

"She believes herself to be my mother, but she does not come to see me, though." Emma played with the fringe of the blanket.

"Be patient. I think he may be the problem – he looked very disbelieving of it all. Are you tired now?"

"Yes."

He helped her up and she took his arm back to her bed, where Nurse Sadlier helped her in and made her comfortable.

She looked sad, lying there, pale against the pillow, a little breathless.

"Emma, give yourself – and them – time. Remember they said they did not know that you were alive."

"Somebody knew I was alive though. If they're telling the truth, somebody told them I was dead! How I hate that person! *Her late mother*, she said!"

Andrew was afraid that a relapse might follow on from such gloomy thoughts, and urged sleep for a while.

CHAPTER FORTY-SIX

"I don't feel able to get up today," she told Nurse Sadlier the following morning.

Emma lay in bed, the curtains drawn about her. But she tried to stay awake; for sleep gave her the same dream over and over – opening a wardrobe, finding her clothes gone, and knowing that she was a prisoner. She tossed and turned upon awakening and finding that she was safe. But if she was safe, why did she still feel like a prisoner?

Andrew visited the following day to find her in bed and in very poor spirits.

"Are you afraid that Spaulding and the Pelican will come after you here?" he asked bluntly. "Because I have news of that pair, which I did not know how to tell you until now. They are dead. The quarrelled over something or other, and inflicted fatal injuries on each other. It was in the Gazette."

"It's a relief they can't harm me. But Andrew, I'm supposed to return to London for the trial of the two women. I don't wish to go."

"Perhaps you can be excused on the grounds of health. Perhaps they will not need your testimony if there are others on hand to testify. Now, you should be able to be happy again; I want to see your smile."

"Andrew, you are very good to me, but I think you would be better off if you forgot me."

He leaped up.

"Are you dismissing me, Emma? Do you feel so little for me?"

"It's not that, Andrew. How can I possibly be able to bring anybody happiness?"

Andrew realised that she was suffering from melancholia, that dreadful affliction for which there was little cure, and he felt very helpless indeed.

"But – do you love me, Emma?"

"Yes, I do. That's why I want your good." She had no more to say and shut her eyes.

Andrew went away distressed, taking his usual woodland path. So occupied was he with his troubles, he missed a turn, and found himself deeper into the woods, lost. He found himself in a small grove, and what was that before him? A tiny, ancient stone church! What a quaint little chapel, tucked away! He entered, and knelt in an oak pew to pray.

There was an old shawled woman in the church, sweeping near the altar. Seeing her struggle to move a heavy chair to brush underneath, he sprang up and moved it for her.

"Thank you, kind young gentleman. I wish you every blessing in your studies, for I see you may be a student."

"I am," he replied.

"And you are here, no doubt, to pray for success in your examinations."

"I would wish so, but at the moment, there is something else – someone else – on my mind. A person dear to me is ill, and I'm afraid she may, through the various sufferings she has been though, which she cannot seem to get out of her mind, be losing her will to live. I speak of a young lady."

The old woman put down her broom and sat in a pew, indicating that he should join her. He poured out his heart as the evening sunlight illuminated the altar. After he had finished, the old woman spoke.

"Your young lady will get over this in time, but she needs something to do. Her mind needs to be busy. I will pray for her, and you will I'm sure get some inspiration."

The day was closing in; he thanked her. She told him how to get back on the main path, and he found it very easily.

CHAPTER FORTY-SEVEN

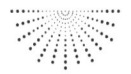

The nurse looked in on her patient and shook her head.

"Is there anything I can do for you, Miss Mayfield?"

"Perhaps you could have a cup of tea with me, for I'm very lonely." Emma said.

The nurse hesitated – she was a servant, but this poor girl had no woman friend to talk to, except Miss Groves, who could not visit often.

"I'll 'ave tea with you, if you'll get up today. Will you get up today?"

Emma paused.

"I will get up today, then."

The nurse had little formal training in her occupation, but she knew that many of her patients needed a caring heart to unburden to, and she was a good listener. Emma prattled on. She cried. She apologised for crying, feeling that she was very weak indeed.

"You have to 'ave your cry-out, Miss." Mrs. Sadlier said flatly. "Don't be ashamed of tears. Didn't our dear Saviour weep sometimes?"

"Yes, He did."

"Well, then. That settles the question. If our Saviour wept, there is no shame in it."

"I think I may have driven Andrew away." she said forlornly.

CHAPTER FORTY-EIGHT

It came to him in a flash the following morning as he opened his book, a book of Russian poetry. He knew how best to help Emma.

He returned the following day with paper, pens and ink. To his relief, Emma was sitting in her chair and looked very happy to see him.

"You need something to do." he said with spirit and determination. "You have a good imagination, I know. You can put it to good use. Write me a story."

Emma's interest was piqued.

"About what?"

"Anything you like – Russian princesses, Earls and Lords falling in love with them –"

"Like where I used to think I came from!" Emma suddenly laughed at the memory.

"You wove quite a tale about it, if I remember."

"A very fanciful one too, but all right, I will write it."

"I will illustrate it when you have finished."

"Really?"

"I look forward to it. But you must sit for the Princess."

She laughed at last, and the sound was music to his ears.

He bought a bundle of firewood in the village for the old woman he had met, and he hoped to find her in or near the church on his return journey. But when he took the path he had been sure he had taken by mistake only a few days ago, he could not find the clearing, or the church. He went over his steps, sure he had made a mistake, and took two other paths just in case, but without success. It was very puzzling.

CHAPTER FORTY-NINE

It was high summer now, and the Castleton garden bloomed beautifully with pink lilies, white gladioli and red begonia. Margaret supplied Lilybell Cottage with the flowers. If only her daughter knew she was only four miles away!

At least the news from Nurse Sadlier was very good. Emma was up and in the garden, writing in the shade of an old elm, some kind of Romance, the nurse said. She even ventured outside the gate, strolling up and down the road. Mr. Groves – the best young man in the world, she was sure – visited her often and Margaret knew that there was a firm attachment there.

If only they could locate Mr. Watkins. Her mother's house had been shut up and sold in the last year, and the servants scattered. Had Mr. Watkins and his wife been the only ones in their household to know what had happened all those years ago in Charlbury?

As Margaret wrapped the bouquet for a servant to take to Lilybell Cottage, a plan formed in her mind. She was not allowed to visit Emma, but burned to tell her about how she had come to be abandoned, and how she and her father were utterly blameless in the matter. She would write it down. Inspired by the news that Emma was writing, she could write her own story and send it or keep it to give to her.

In her morning room the following day, she began.

Once upon a time there was a man with deep blue eyes named Arthur Castleton and a young woman named Margaret Norris. She fell in love with him at a dance given by a mutual neighbour. They danced four dances, causing a lot of talk, and afterwards, he asked if he might call upon her. Her mother did not approve of him, for he had a brusque manner, and never cared what others thought of him. He was not a fawning, deceiving sort of man, such as Margaret had met before. She liked honesty and candour. But Margaret was an heiress and her mother thought that Arthur was a fortune-hunter.

One day the lovebirds went out riding together and were caught in a spring thunderstorm. They took refuge in his room at Oxford, which happened to be very near. Cold and shivering, Margaret asked for a glass of wine. He joined her, and Margaret demanded her glass be filled with more. Again, he joined her. She huddled close to him, for lightening frightened her dreadfully. She suddenly kissed him, and she forgot her fear of thunderstorms. Nothing existed for her except those deep blue eyes of Arthur Castleton.

What every mother fears for her daughter happened. They lay together.

"I am sorry," Arthur said. "I feel I may have taken advantage."

"I do not feel that you did." Margaret said. "I – we should not have drank all that wine. I lost my head."

"I will marry you."

"You are an honourable man, Arthur. But you do not have to unless of course –"

"I want to marry you, Margaret, child or no child! I love you."

"And I love you. But we will have to keep our engagement secret; my mother doesn't understand you."

"Because I always say what I think, instead of being polite? Drawing room manners bore me."

"Give her time, Arthur. She will come around, when she sees how I feel about you."

Two months later Margaret knew she must be enceinte. She confessed to her mother, who was very angry. Mrs. Norris put the blame squarely on Arthur – he had brought her to his room with the intention of seducing her, and plied her with wine! Margaret was too ashamed to tell her mother that she had asked for the wine and had kissed him first.

"You must not be in any hurry to marry such an odious man," said Mrs. Norris. "Do not make up your mind until after the child is born. He is a stubborn, selfish man and his behaviour must improve before he becomes a part of this family."

"But how am I to hide the baby from society?" Margaret asked, perplexed.

"I will arrange it. You and the child can go to my sister's in Liverpool."

Margaret's pains began on December 23rd, and her baby was born the day after at about four in the evening, just as darkness gathered.

"Mamma, she is beautiful!" she cried out, holding out her arms for the child. "I'm naming her Emma."

"You must rest now, Margaret. You can hold the baby later. I will give her to the nurse."

Margaret fell asleep. When she awoke about midnight, it was completely dark and only a candle illuminated the room. She heard church bells, and saw her mother sitting by her side.

"Margaret, I am deeply sorry. It couldn't be helped, child. Poor little Emma expired. The doctor has been here and certified her death."

Margaret's heart broke in two at the news. She was utterly shattered.

"Mamma, bring her to me, so that I can hold her and kiss her, and tell her that I love her!"

"Oh dear Margaret, I have already had her taken away. Remember her as you saw her this morning, healthy and pink, your dear little Emma."

The next days were dreadful for the young mother. She kept Christmas from her bedchamber as much as she could. She put her hands to her ears to shut out the sounds of the bells, the carol-singing and the New Year celebrations. From now on, she would hate Christmas and New Year! She was offered cherries, plum pudding, Yule log and bonbons to cheer her up, but she shooed the well-meaning servants away.

After her lying-in, Arthur came to see her. They held each other in their grief. He told her of the funeral. He had not seen his daughter either, and was very regretful that he had never held her. After that he came often, in spite of Mrs. Norris telling him that Margaret was not well enough to receive visitors.

"You are lying, woman." he had said with contempt, as he'd pushed his way in past the door and took the stairs three steps at a time.

He and Margaret decided to get married as soon as possible; they could not bear to be apart. Mrs. Norris strenuously objected, so they eloped one night. There was nothing she could do about it! Margaret was Mrs. Castleton. She hardly spoke for three months, so shocked was she.

They set up house in Oxford, as Arthur's profession was in the University. They had three sons and no other daughter. Neither Arthur nor Margaret like Christmas and if it were not for their children, would turn their backs upon it completely.

Margaret put down her pen. There was more to write, but it would wait. She blotted the sheets and when the ink was dry rolled them and tied them with pink ribbon.

Where, oh where was Mr. Watkins?

CHAPTER FIFTY

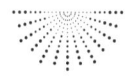

Emma had asked Andrew to get her a book on Russian life and culture so that her story would be authentic. She wrote and wrote and wrote – it began with the mink-clad Princess Olga being driven by sleigh and six white horses barely visible against the snow on her way to St. Petersburg to attend her first Ball, then the dashing Princes and Officers whose proposals she turned down one after another, then, having attended the Ballet, her secret dancing lessons from a French Master. When Emma was not writing, she was reading the book, choosing names for her characters and taking note of Russian customs, which she kept in a notebook.

She was feeling better. The doctor confirmed that she was not consumptive, and Andrew rejoiced. He had spent most of the summer at Oxford instead of returning home. He would be completely happy now if his mother would accept that there was no other girl for him except Emma Mayfield. But his mother, having given up on the Edisons, had put her eye on Miss Williams, the daughter of the attorney who was supposed to be Emma's guardian, but who did not care one whit for her. Williams was openly now one of the attorneys for Baggotts of Birmingham.

"Poor Mother!" he said to Ophelia. "She doesn't know that I and Mr. Williams exchanged angry words last Christmas, and that I would be the very last man he would allow his daughter to marry. How can I get Mother to understand that I love Emma?"

"I truly don't know the answer to that, it would require Mother - and Father - too to have a change of heart. And did you tell me that those two dreadful women in London have been sentenced to fifteen years transportation? Now they'll know what it feels like to be imprisoned and sent away. Justice."

CHAPTER FIFTY-ONE

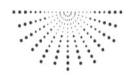

The leaves were falling and November came in. Emma finished her story. After a dramatic showdown in 10 Downing Street between the Russian diplomats and the Prime Minister, which almost ended in a duel, the loving couple escaped into anonymity and went to live in an island off the coast of Scotland.

But what of their secret child? Every Christmas gift held a clue as to her real identity. Her loving Aunt deciphered them and found out she was of Royal blood on one side and Aristocratic blood on the other, and sought to protect her from her enemies...for she was a heiress of great wealth. The story grew and grew, and Andrew read it avidly whenever he visited, complaining that she had always left off at a cliffhanger.

"I cannot wait until you get to me," he grinned. "Who shall I be? Can I be an artist, under the patronage of the Queen? Can I be your true love?"

"You are my true love," she replied, to his delight.

Not five miles away, Mrs. Castleton took up her pen again to write the second part of her story.

One day in November 1856 Margaret got an urgent message from her mother's coachman, Mr. Watkins. Mrs. Norris had been unwell for some time, but had taken a bad turn and wished to see her as a matter of great urgency. Margaret donned her cloak and muff and Mr. Watkins drove the horses hard until they came to Norris Estate. She entered her mother's bedroom to find her in a state of great agitation. She had had the Last Rites of the Church and expected to die at any moment. The priest had departed, and Mrs. N dismissed her nurse.

"Margaret, Margaret! I have a great confession to make to you, and I fear you will not forgive me for it!"

Margaret was very alarmed to hear this, and did not know what course this conversation would take. She loved her mother, as did her boys. Arthur had never really thawed.

"Margaret, this is so hard for me to say, but I must say it! I have done you a terrible wrong!"

"Mother, what is it? Tell me?"

"Your baby Emma lived. She did not die. I made it up, to put a break between you and Arthur. Oh I wish I had not done it! How I wish!"

Margaret froze in her chair, hardly daring to believe what she had heard. Was her mother insane? Had her illness affected her mind?

"Tell me more, Mother!" She had grasped her mother's arms.

"Hurt me as much as you wish, Margaret, I will deserve it! I had Emma taken away and left in the churchyard of St. Michael's at Earlsbury. She was found – I made sure that she would be. I am a bad woman but would not have murder on my conscience!"

Margaret got up and paced the floor, but she felt weak and had to support herself against the chair.

"Where is she?"

"Still in Earlsbury. She was adopted by a childless widow who looks after her very well. I have sent her a Birthday gift every Christmas of her life, anonymously, left by the Mayfield grave."

Margaret walked about, now she was in a state of great agitation.

"I still don't understand, Mother. How could you keep it from me?"

"When I realised that you and Arthur had married, it sent me into a state of deep shock. What you interpreted as my distress at your marriage, was more distress at what I had done to your child. I wanted to tell you – but did not know how! You would hate me! Arthur would have exacted a miserable revenge, turned me out of your life, perhaps taken me to Court for kidnapping and ruined me and the entire family! I have endured nearly seventeen years of agony, of guilt, of sleeplessness – how I have been punished, and I deserve it!

"Then, last year – when Watkins left the gift – for it was he who had the commission of taking it – she was there, at the churchyard, to receive it. She demanded to know who she was, where she was from – he could not tell her of course. She flung the gift back at him and told him to come no more! When I heard that, I went to confess my sins, and Father Ellington told me I had to tell you. I have been trying to find words all the year. Now, I am about to die. Will God forgive me? Father Ellington says He will, but I must try to repair the harm I have done in the little time left to me!

Margaret believed her mother, but was unable to make sense of her own confusion and feelings, the joy that her child was alive existed at the same time as the anger at her mother for what she had done. She knew that when she told her husband, he would explode in fury, and so hasten her mother's death – something she did not want to feel responsible for. In her great turmoil, she summoned Watkins. He denied it, perhaps afraid that he could be charged in the kidnapping. No such thing had happened; the old woman must be raving. Margaret could get nothing from him. After her mother's death, he quit the house and the area immediately.

Unfortunately, no more information was possible from her mother. Margaret told her that she forgave her before she died, though she still felt anger – and still does at what her mother did.

After Mrs. Norris died, Margaret began to be occupied with thoughts of Emma perhaps going to the churchyard at Christmas Eve that year. She would be there! But she had to tell Arthur now. His reaction was predictable. He was angry, astounded and unbelieving. Nevertheless, he humoured her. They drove to St. Michael's Churchyard in Earlsbury on Christmas Eve, not knowing where to look, only watching for a young woman who expected to meet somebody. Instead, they found a chaotic situation as a young woman was known to have fallen very ill upon the grave of a Mrs. Mayfield. This was evidence that they had found Emma.

The Ending to this story is not written. Arthur is searching for proof, or at least, strong evidence that this Emma is his daughter. Watkins and his wife remain at large. He has moved from the address that Mrs. Norris' attorneys had for him.

Thank God, Emma is recovering! My darling daughter Emma – for I am Margaret Castleton – lives!

She decided that she would have the pages bound as a little book, and would add a great deal of information about the family, the birthdates of her brothers, and the names of her cousins.

CHAPTER FIFTY-TWO

1858

Emma was almost completely recovered now, but could not stay very long out in the cold, for the doctor warned that this winter in particular she would be in need of warmth and nourishing food. He did not want her to catch as much as a sniffle. Her clothes were beginning to fit her once again instead of hanging off her as if she were a skeleton.

Gifts arrived – a warm merino cloak with hood, a fur muff, strong boots. Mrs. Castleton sent them. She had already sent over materials and patterns for winter gowns.

"I should be grateful to her," Emma said to Andrew, as she sewed the seam for her gown. "Instead, I'm resentful. Why does she not come? I haven't even had a note from her! Why this coldness? I would as soon not hear from her at all, and make my own way, than for her to tantalise me like this."

Andrew reminded her that Mr. Castleton might be the cause.

"As we are speaking of mothers," he said, coughing a little. "My mother is insisting that I return home for Christmas, at least for part of the holidays. The little ones are forgetting me, she says."

"And so you should be at home for Christmas."

"But I hate to leave you alone, Emma."

"You know I would as soon ignore Christmas, Andrew, as keep it. I'm going to pretend it's just any other day of the year."

"Ophelia offered to come up to help me shop for the family, we'll come to see you on your eighteenth Birthday then, before I leave Oxford. You're not ignoring your birthday, I hope."

Emma was silent as she bit the thread with her teeth. He awaited her reply in vain as she began to rummage in her sewing box. Still no reply.

Andrew rose and stamped his foot on the ground.

"Emma, answer me. And perhaps it is time to quell the self-pity! I must tell you it doesn't become anybody, especially a girl who has much to be grateful for, as you have."

"What did you say?" she exclaimed, rising from the table.

"Yes, you're bitter and resentful. You came through great hardship, almost died and recovered your health with the attention and the help of your friends, and cannot see anything to be happy about. You have your life in front of you. You can continue in your bitterness, or you can begin to be grateful for what you have, and grateful too for the people who love you! The choice is before you!"

"Go away, and there is no need for you to return!" she said to him with anger. "You're better off without me in any case, you and your family! Forget me!" She turned her back on him to rummage again in her box.

Andrew got his hat and coat and stormed out. She rushed to the window and watched him stride out the gate. He looked behind, and she caught his eye, and she looked down, in remorse. He turned again and walked off.

She went back to her sewing, but his words had stung, and her own reaction had stung her worse.

CHAPTER FIFTY-THREE

"Margaret!" Mr. Castleton waved a letter at the breakfast table. "Watkins is found!"

"Oh thank God! Thank God! Tell me!"

"He and Mrs. Watkins have retired to Lyme Regis in Dorset and his attorney writes that he may be willing to talk with us, on a certain condition."

"Who's Watkins?" asked young Arthur, aged sixteen.

"Your grandmother's coachman."

"Why is it important that he is found?" asked twelve-year old Michael.

"Did he run away with Grandmamma's coach and horses?" asked Timothy, eight, a spoonful of red jam halfway to his mouth.

"No, he didn't. They were sold, you silly little boy," said Michael.

"I'm not silly and stop calling me little!" Timothy, using the spoon as a catapult to fire the jam was successful in landing most of it upon his brother's chin.

Michael thought that an unexpected helping of jam on his face was a benefit to his morning and tried to reach it with his tongue, making Timothy lunge to steal it back, which resulted in both boys overturning their chairs and ending up rolling on the carpet in a tangle of limbs.

Young Arthur shrugged and took a book out of his pocket and propped it up against the coffeepot. Table manners this morning were non-existent and his father and mother had not even noticed. It must be something dashed important, and he'd no doubt he'd be told of it in time.

CHAPTER FIFTY-FOUR

"The very fact that he wishes to talk to us, proves that he has something to say," Margaret said when she and Arthur had retired to the library for some privacy. "Do we really need to speak with him at all?"

"I think it wisest. I will leave immediately for Dorsetshire. We will not of course pursue any justice. The perpetrator of the crime is no longer with us." He sounded bitter.

"Arthur, please listen to me. Do not say anything that will cause him to be afraid of you and clam up. I will come also. The boys can go to my sister's."

"Oh! All right."

"What will we tell the boys, Arthur? They have an older sister but what a humiliation to admit that she was born before we were even married! How are we to explain it?"

Her husband got that fierce look that made his dark blue eyes steely. He took her by the shoulders, firmly.

"One thing I am positive about, Margaret. No more lies in our family."

"I think that is best also," said Margaret.

Meantime the servant could not understand how everything she touched on one side of the table was sticky. La, what had happened? And why was the master shouting to his man to pack his valise?

CHAPTER FIFTY-FIVE

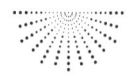

Andrew's words had hurt Emma and she hoped that he would not take them seriously. She thought about them all morning, and every time she replayed them in her mind, they stung more. That was what Andrew thought of her! She prayed fervently to God to help her to become a more grateful, optimistic person.

Her gown was almost finished.

"Would it greatly disturb you, Miss Mayfield, if we were to get this room ready for Christmas?" Mrs. Sadlier, whose occupation had changed from nursing to housekeeping, was before her with an armful of paper.

"Oh, Christmas? I suppose it would be all right," Emma replied, trying to be cheerful.

"I'll get my grandchildren here to help," Mrs. Sadlier said. "And Mr. Sadlier is bringing a tree."

Lilybell Cottage was invaded by at least six children aged from fourteen to four, and supervised by their grandparents, the living room began to be transformed. Caught up in the children's excitement, Emma began to remember the Christmasses of the past, when she had been enthusiastic, and remembering how she had avidly looked forward to her gifts, and had to be reminded, like every child, that Christmas was about the greatest Gift of all to the world, Jesus. She remembered too the old woman in the alley and what she had said.

She saw a small child reach for scissors, and intervened. "I'll cut the paper for you," she said, quickly getting on her knees beside him. "Now look, we'll make one little cut here, and when we shake it out it will look so lovely!" Then another scratched herself on the holly, and cried, so she comforted her. She felt almost happy again, and almost forgot the spat between her and Andrew.

The decorations were among the plainest that Emma had ever seen, there were no toys or twinkling lights, but they had a simple charm that she found much more to her taste. Baggots of Birmingham could keep their gas lamps and mechanical tricks! Before she knew it she was inventing a story about the decorations chatting to one another, quarrelling over who was the most beautiful, and she had a little circle around her, enthralled, while Mrs. Sadlier served lemonade and biscuits in the light of a blazing log fire. After that, they sang *'Away in a Manger.'*

"You 'ave a way with children, Miss Mayfield," said Mrs. Sadlier after they had left. "I'll be 'earing nothing else from them now but the red papers envying the green, and the fir cones preening themselves to look better than the holly!"

CHAPTER FIFTY-SIX

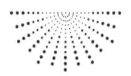

Andrew did not come on Christmas Eve morning. Emma bowed her head and cried. She'd sent him away, and now she bitterly regretted it. She was eighteen years old today and found no joy in it.

How long was she to stay here, without any friends, any society, anything to amuse her? Her book was written – Andrew had illustrated it and taken it to a printer he knew who was training apprentices and would make one hundred copies. It would then be bound. But in the book, Olga and Andrei had declared their undying love and now look what had happened!

The deserted living-room seemed to mock her today. She ate her breakfast in silence. She did not want to stay here any longer. She would leave in the New Year. No, she would leave before that. She would leave today.

Where would she go? There was an Inn not far away, she would begin there. After Christmas she would advertise herself as a nursery maid. She loved children and loved to amuse them. It was something. She'd ask Mrs. Sadlier for a reference. She'd tell her how to write a good one. She has some money, for the Castletons also sent her an allowance.

The Castletons! She was heartily sick of being on the edges of their lives, hidden from view! She shamed them, that she knew. The fact that they would not even communicate with her made her angry.

"It's a justified anger," she said as she attached a piece of Limerick lace to the neck of her gown. *"They keep me, their relative, their daughter I am sure – at arm's length! For how much longer? I'm heartily sick of the Castletons! As soon as I've eaten my dinner today, I'm going out from here and I'll make my own way in life and I'll never hear from them and they will never hear from me again. As for Andrew – I have hurt him – I sent him away - I'm not for him."*

CHAPTER FIFTY-SEVEN

Andrew replayed Emma's words over and over in his mind, remembering her dismissal with great hurt. He did not feel he had the choice of going to wish her a Happy Birthday, so he and Ophelia had left for Earlsbury on the 23rd. He was heartbroken and Ophelia was downcast. She felt strongly that he should have gone to see Emma on her birthday, no matter what she'd said.

He received a rapturous welcome in Villiers Street. The younger children threw themselves on him, so happy to see their big strong brother again, that he felt guilty about not having spent most of the summer with them. He carried them around, one under each arm, until his mother told him that it was quite enough. She had news for him. Tomorrow,

Mrs. Todd was calling in with her children, and he was to make himself very agreeable to Misses Lucy or Julia, whichever took his fancy the most, for Mrs. Todd's brother had married the daughter of Baronet Elliott in Kent.

Andrew said nothing but the joy drained from his face.

"Mother, may I please speak with you," Ophelia said quietly as they prepared the sherry trifle later in the kitchen. Gracie was upstairs warming the beds.

"I suppose you are to admonish me, Philly."

"If only you would accept Andrew's choice of wife, it would make him so happy."

"Impossible. You know what she is. She will bring nothing with her."

"Why does that matter so much? She's God's child as much as you or me! It's Christmas, Mamma. When the lowly shepherds came to see the Infant King, what did they have to bring? Has not Jesus taught us that high position and wealth don't matter, are not we, his followers, supposed to see deeper than that? Andrew loves Emma. He always has. You do him a grave injustice. I am sorry, Mamma, for saying all this, but I had to. I love you." She kissed her mother's cheek.

Her mother was very quiet, but a tear rolled down her cheek. Her father appeared in the doorway, he had heard all.

"You know what the world is like, Philly. We can accept Emma, but will the Williams', the Sheltons, the Todds? And what of the families who send their children to be educated by me? It's not us that's wrong, Philly, it's the world."

"But are we not expected to take the higher road, Papa? If those people cut you because of Andrew's choice of wife, are they really worth knowing? Why should Emma suffer all of her life from something over which she had no control? As for your pupils, if their parents remove them, you will get more – you will, because you're an excellent teacher.

"Please, tell Andrew you accept Emma. And send him back to Forest Hill today on her birthday!"

CHAPTER FIFTY-EIGHT

E mma made herself ready. She had laid her clothes in a box and wore her new red and green plaid gown, which was the warmest in her possession. She donned her cloak and laced her boots. She would slip away while Mrs. Sadlier took her afternoon nap.

"Now, Emma," she said to herself, and raised her head to look out the window to make sure she could escape unseen.

To her dismay, snow had begun to fall, silent and steady, it had crept up on the village, and had already made a thick, white carpet on the road outside, and covered the roofs of the cottages opposite.

Emma sat heavily upon the bed. She would have to wait until after Christmas, and she did not feel like waiting. She heard the sound of a carriage halt outside. She peered out. It had stopped just outside the gate, and there were several people getting out. A man first, who looked about briefly, who helped a woman out. Then three boys appeared to tumble out one after another. A coachman began to unload several brightly coloured packages. They were wealthy, these people.

The Castletons. It must be the Castletons. Her heart beat fast. She watched them as she came in the gate and heard their knock upon the door. She heard their voices then. She took off her cloak. Should she show herself? Who else were they here to see, if not her, Emma Mayfield?

Looking at herself in the mirror, she arranged a stray curl. Then she pulled herself up straight and opened the door to her new life.

CHAPTER FIFTY-NINE

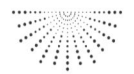

They surrounded her, these Castletons, and lost no time in telling her who they were.

"I'm your mother, Emma." The lady in the fur-trimmed green velvet cloak had soft brown eyes, full of tears and tenderness. "This is your father." The man looked rather distant, or dazed, and bowed. "And these boys are your brothers." The boys bowed. They were on their best behaviour. They had a grown up sister and the news was stunning to them, but they rather liked the idea too.

"I shall bring you all hot chocolate," Mrs. Sadlier said.

Emma surveyed them all. She and her mother sat on the sofa. Her mother took both her hands in hers and began to tell Emma about the first hours of her life, while her father sat in a nearby chair, listening, not speaking a word. Emma felt shy of him. Not so the boys, who after drinking their chocolate, were sent out to enjoy the snow for a while, and they were already pelting each other with snowballs.

Mrs. Castleton caressed her daughter's hands. She had said everything upon her heart. She drew a little bound notebook from her reticule. "What I have not said to you, I have written here." she said.

Emma was weeping, but through her tears, she smiled.

"I have invented quite a history of you both," she said. "You shall be mightily entertained, I think, when you have read it!"

They both laughed, and her father spoke then.

"I'm not very good at this sort of thing," he said. "But rest assured, you were loved from the first. I mourned you and when I carried your – or the little coffin - to the grave, I shed tears as any father would."

"But who was in the coffin?" Emma asked quietly, now very affected.

"Watkins said that the undertaker was paid to place a rolled-up blanket within."

Emma felt the familiar anger well up within her at her maternal grandmother, and saw that her father felt the same way.

"Mother repented deeply. I pray she is at peace!" said Mrs. Castleton quietly.

"I hope so too," Emma said then, making a great effort. "It's Christmas." She glanced at her father, and saw too, his eyes, which were so like her own, soften. He nodded gravely, clasping and unclasping his hands.

"We will endeavour to forget all the harm she did now." he said in a rather authoritative voice.

"Mamma! There's a man come on a horse!" Timothy, covered in snow, had run in.

Emma got to her feet when she saw Andrew, his greatcoat covered in snow, charge into the room. His anxious eyes sought hers immediately. She ran to embrace him, snow and all. He held her tightly for a long time. They did not see the Castletons exchange a tender, happy glance. They knew love when they saw it.

"Mother sent this," he said then, hardly noticing the Castletons in his joy to see her, and the joy at his reception. He thrust a letter into her hand.

"It's one of those new Christmas cards," she said, opening it. "The first one I have ever received. I will read it in full later. But she says that she hopes I am well recovered and – will visit her soon?" She thought of the last time she and Andrew's mother had met. It had been a bad meeting. Could they begin again? Why not? Was not life full of new beginnings, if we allow our hearts to lead us? She thought of dear Aunt Jane, who had shown her the love of a mother, and Grandmother Grey, celebrating the Feast in Heaven. She blinked back more tears.

It was getting dark. The boys had come in and Mrs. Castleton suggested they gather in front of the Crib to sing carols.

"What shall we begin with?" asked Mr. Castleton.

"*O Come All Ye Faithful*" suggested Tim.

As they gathered close and sang together, Emma saw through the window, in the whitened twilight, the figure of an old woman, wrapped up well against the weather, standing by the gate. She had wispy white hair showing from under her close bonnet. She seemed to be looking directly at her and smiling.

'Goodness me' thought Emma, with a wild feeling in her heart. *'She looks very like* – '

Andrew followed her eye to the window.

"That's the woman from the old church in the woods!" he whispered to Emma with astonishment.

"Who?"

"I met her, in the woods one day. But when I went back to find her, she was gone."

"But I'm sure I met her too –"

They gazed at each other briefly, understanding and not understanding.

"She must be in need of firewood or something –" he whispered, starting up.

"She has left!" Emma said. The woman was nowhere to be seen. They knew that even if they went out to find her, that they would not even see her footsteps. They resumed their singing.

"O Sing Choirs of Angels

Sing in Exultation!

Sing all ye citizens of Heaven and Earth.

Glory to God

In the Highest!

O Come let us Adore Him.

O Come let us Adore Him.

O Come let us Adore Him.

Christ the Lord!"

∽

THANK YOU FOR CHOOSING A PUREREAD BOOK!

We hope you enjoyed the story, and as a way to thank you for choosing PureRead we'd like to send you this free book, and other fun reader rewards...

Click here for your free copy of Whitechapel Waif
PureRead.com/victorian

Thanks again for reading.
See you soon!

OUR GIFT TO YOU

AS A WAY TO SAY THANK YOU WE WOULD LOVE TO SEND YOU THIS BEAUTIFUL STORY FREE OF CHARGE.

Click here for your free copy of Whitechapel Waif

PureRead.com/victorian

At PureRead we publish books you can trust. Great tales without smut or swearing, but with all of the mystery and romance you expect from a great story.

Be the first to know when we release new books, take part in our fun competitions, and get surprise free books in your inbox by signing up to our free VIP Reader list.

As a thank you you'll receive a copy of Whitechapel Waif straight away in you inbox.

Click here for your free copy of Whitechapel Waif

PureRead.com/victorian

Printed in Great Britain
by Amazon